HEINOUS

HEINOUS

FACES OF EVIL

DEBRA WEBB

PINK
HOUSE
PRESS

Copyright © 2014 Debra Webb, Pink House Press

Edited by Marijane Diodati

Cover Design by Kendel Flaum

PINK HOUSE PRESS
WebbWorks
Huntsville, Alabama

First Edition July 2014

ISBN 10: 1497395976
ISBN 13: 9781497395978

"…nothing can satisfy it but the blood…
how heinous, how sinful must the evil be…"
William Throsby Bridges

CHAPTER ONE

CHAPEL ROAD
BIRMINGHAM, ALABAMA,
SUNDAY, SEPTEMBER 5, 9:30 A.M.

Deputy Chief Jess Harris was well aware the car had stopped moving. She was also reasonably sure the detective behind the wheel had said something, but his words didn't register. The events of the last week kept cycling through her thoughts as if she'd missed something and should have recognized it by now.

Whatever *it* was, it lingered just outside her mental grasp. She should get out of the car and do her job. After all, this was a crime scene and inside that century old chapel was a homicide victim who deserved her full attention.

Still, she hesitated.

The truth was, considering all that had happened in the past six days, a wiser woman might have done what everyone had been urging her to do for weeks now—to go into hiding by accepting the offer of protective custody the Bureau had made at least twice already.

Right. If only the solution were that simple.

The Joint Task Force comprised of the FBI, Interpol, and the Birmingham Police Department were frantically attempting to find and stop the sociopathic serial killer known as the Player to no avail. Unfortunately, they were no closer than they had been last month or the month before that.

Eric Spears. The Player.

The name echoed inside her.

For more than five years, the FBI had been tracking him without success. Supervisory Special Agent Ralph Gant, Jess's superior at Quantico during most of her former career with the Bureau, was lead on the Joint Task Force.

Giving the Task Force grace, this wasn't the first time the Bureau or Jess had faced this level of evil, or had such difficulty catching a killer. Spears never left a trail to follow, not so much as a trace that would lead to him. As elusive as he proved, his motives and methods were well documented. He liked to play games with his victims and each game was always the same.

Until now.

Now his true goal appeared to be…*her.*

Recruiting followers to do his bidding, he had targeted people closest to Jess as well as significant places in her life, and then his twisted game had suddenly taken a new turn.

Anger tightened her chest.

He had delved deep into her past and touched the few cherished memories she possessed of her early childhood. He'd taken those happy snippets of the too short time with her parents and turned them into something malevolent, goading Jess with the idea that nothing about who she was or where she came from was as it seemed.

Psychopath and Spears follower, Amanda Brownfield, and her rural home in Scottsboro were the latest pieces of this new puzzle. Jess had expected to spend this sweltering Sunday before Labor Day at the place local deputies had dubbed the body farm. Images of all those unmarked open graves along with the metal box that held photos of victims filtered through her mind, mocking Jess with life-shattering allegations about her father.

She simply couldn't wrap her head around the theory that her father had lived a secret life with a multi-generational family of killers. As disturbing as that possibility was, part of her sensed there was a kernel of truth buried within all the lies and victims at the Brownfield body farm.

Whatever that truth turned out to be, the game was escalating...rushing toward a conclusion precisely orchestrated by Eric Spears.

How many others would lose their lives before it was over?

At this very moment, there were three young women whose lives hung in the balance. Two had been identified, the third they'd only learned about twenty-four hours ago. The photo of the latest victim was running on all media outlets. No one had come forward to identify her as of yet. She wasn't in any databases. No criminal history. Just another young woman with the look—tall and beautiful with long dark hair—that made her the target of a serial killer at the very top level of the evil scale.

Whatever Spears had in store for these women, he appeared to be collecting rather than murdering them. This additional abrupt change in his MO provided Jess with a glimmer of hope that these victims—unlike all his others—might be found alive.

With a deep bolstering breath, she let go of those troubling thoughts and focused on the here and now. Sergeant Chet Harper had called with the address of a homicide the Special Problems Unit, BPD's hybrid major crimes division, had caught from dispatch. The sooner she was finished here, the sooner she could get back to the case haunting her.

"Ready, Chief?" Lieutenant Clint Hayes, her ride this morning, asked.

Jess slipped her eyeglasses into place and reached for the door handle. "As ready as I'll ever be, Lieutenant."

Emerging from Hayes's Audi, Jess surveyed the wooded setting. Department cruisers blocked off access at both ends of the street. Yellow crime scene tape surrounded the quaint old chapel that had long ago been a thriving congregation, but now served as a wedding venue for those who preferred a vintage setting. A few parking slots away the BPD Crime Scene van waited.

She and Hayes had passed a pair of uniforms canvassing the neighbors, most of whom were probably too far away to have witnessed anything, but that was the extent of visible official activity.

Jess rounded the hood, meeting Hayes on the sidewalk. "Harper and Wells are inside?"

"They are." He paused for her to start up the walk ahead of him. "ME's en route."

Jess surveyed the towering stained glass windows as she climbed the steps at the chapel's front entrance. If the trouble had begun outside the chapel, there were no visible indications. Hayes opened the towering doors and Jess walked inside. The coppery scent of blood hung in the air. Sergeant Chet Harper and Detective Lori Wells waited in the small vestibule.

"What do we have so far, Sergeant?" Jess retrieved gloves and shoe covers from her bag.

"We asked the evidence techs to wait until you arrived."

Lori picked up where Harper left off. "We felt you should see this before anything was disturbed."

Unease nudged Jess. She dismissed it. "In that case, let's not keep the victim waiting any longer."

The detectives stepped apart, allowing a view into the sanctuary. Rows of pews lined each side of the center aisle that led to the altar. In front of the altar, a man knelt in prayer. *The victim.*

A trail of coagulated blood stained the worn pine planks of the chapel floor. As Jess moved toward the man whose blood had made that path, the two large urns standing on the altar before him captured her attention. Both urns were filled with peace lilies.

Jess's instincts sharpened. She'd hated those damned things since she was ten years old and sat on the front pew with her sister at their parents' funeral. A new tension trickled through her, but she set it aside. No reason to jump to conclusions since the lilies might very well be part of the wedding arrangements.

Only one way to find out. "Tell me about the flowers."

"The floral delivery for the wedding isn't scheduled until two this afternoon," Lori said, confirming the deduction Jess had hoped wouldn't pan out.

"We believe the killer brought them," Harper added, "to set the scene."

If the lilies were from the killer, her detectives understood what that meant. *Spears.* In all his infernal digging around in Jess's past, he had discovered her aversion to peace lilies. This wasn't the first time he'd used them to send her a message. He wanted to shake her, to throw her off balance in preparation for his final move.

Despite his detailed planning, Spears's one mistake was vastly underestimating her determination to see him in hell.

Jess circled then crouched in front of the victim to have a closer look. Whatever else Spears had planned, understanding how each new twist connected to his end game was the only way to potentially block his next move.

The victim's face was ashen with death. Eyes were open. Lips were sutured closed. Palms were pressed

6

together, glued most likely, as if in prayer. Something like piano wire fastened around his neck kept his arms in the proper position. The wire had cut into his flesh, leaving a ring of blood around his collar. A steel rod shoved down the back of his shirt and trousers, exiting at the crotch and piercing the wood floor kept his torso upright. Nails secured his feet to the floor.

The primary source of blood appeared to have drained from the groin area, probably a femoral artery judging by the amount.

"Considering the state of rigor," Harper said as he crouched next to Jess, "he's been dead several hours. Lividity suggests he's been in this position the whole time."

"He was still alive when the suturing was done." Jess indicated the streams of blood painting his chin and throat. "You have an ID yet?"

"Gordon Henshaw, seventy-five, retired pastor," Lori listed. "He does the occasional wedding and funeral now. He was scheduled to perform the ceremony here this evening. The two wedding coordinators found him when they arrived around eight this morning to start decorating. Cook is taking their statements now."

Officer Chad Cook was the youngest member of the team. He'd been prepping for the detective's exam recently. Jess looked forward to making that promotion happen for him. With most days spent investigating murder cases, she appreciated those rare opportunities when work included something to celebrate.

Unless this man's murder put them a step closer to stopping Spears, there would be absolutely nothing to celebrate today.

"You have an address?" The vic wasn't wearing a wedding band. "Any close family?"

"We have his address. Don't know about family yet." Harper looked directly at Jess then. "Henshaw spent forty years as pastor of an Irondale congregation. The small church near the house where you lived with your parents."

As if the news triggered some switch that opened the gate to long forgotten memories, the smell of cherry pipe tobacco, a deep, gentle voice and a slow, easy smile whispered through Jess's mind. *Pastor Gordon.*

He'd patched up her skinned knee once and given her a stern talking to another time. He'd promised that God was always watching and keeping his children safe.

Not exactly the way things turned out, Pastor.

Damn. Jess pushed to her feet. "Let's track down any relatives or friends who might have been in contact with him in the past twenty-four to forty-eight hours." She glanced around the sanctuary for another door. "Is there an office? Bridal chamber? Where are Cook and the coordinators?"

"In the office," Lori explained. "The reception hall, office, and wedding party rooms are in a separate building around back."

"I'll get the evidence techs started." Harper headed for the front entrance.

Hayes reached for his cell. "I'm on the family and friends."

Jess studied the reverend for a moment longer. The notion that she should call her sister made a fleeting appearance amid her other thoughts. She and Lily hadn't seen this man in more than thirty years—not since their parents died. He was a homicide victim, her new case. Basically a stranger...*who was dead because of her.*

Between the blood and the cloying scent of the flowers, Jess needed air. "Is there a back door?"

"There is, but it's locked. No signs of forced entry. The chapel director is at another venue trying to relocate tonight's wedding and she has the only key." Lori gestured to the front entrance. "The killer had to come through that door."

"Let's find out what Cook has learned in the interviews." Jess hoped they could make next of kin notification before the media got wind of this murder. Any minute now, the newshounds would arrive. The best reporters always had their sources within any law enforcement agency. It was a miracle they weren't on the scene already.

She followed Lori through the vestibule and out into the humid air. It shouldn't be this damned hot in September, especially before noon. A couple of deep breaths helped to clear the stench of death from her lungs. One of the more unpleasant side effects of the first trimester of pregnancy was the inability to ignore the pungent odors associated with investigating a murder scene.

"Please tell me this is not going to keep you and Dan away from Daddy's barbecue."

The ME had arrived.

Dr. Sylvia Baron, Jefferson County's Assistant Corner, paused on the walkway.

With yet another person connected to her or her past murdered, Jess summoned what she hoped was a respectable smile. "Wouldn't miss it."

"Good." Sylvia removed her sunglasses and scrutinized the entrance to the chapel. "I can't remember the last time I was in church on a Sunday morning. I hope the roof doesn't fall in."

Somehow the ME's self-deprecating wit lessened the tension nagging at Jess. "If it didn't fall in on me," she offered, "you're probably safe."

"Good point, Harris."

Jess watched the medical examiner, who was also her friend, stride toward the entrance. As usual, she was dressed impeccably, from the top of her recently colored auburn tresses to her shiny lilac stilettoes that exactly matched the classic sheath she wore. Sylvia could be a little abrasive with a sharp tongue she used on Jess as often as not, but the ME was the best at what she did. Jess had a feeling that beneath that brash attitude was a woman who only wanted to protect the soft heart she adamantly denied possessing.

Maybe they were more alike than Jess preferred to acknowledge on most days.

A warning that she'd received a text message came from deep within her bag. News about a break in the hunt for Spears or a full confession from Amanda Brownfield would be nice. Barely thirty-six hours ago, Amanda had been taken into custody. It was likely too early to expect any additional revelations from her.

Spears's newest follower claimed to be Jess's half sister. Worse, Amanda had abandoned her four-year-old daughter on a street in downtown Birmingham for no other reason than being asked to do so by Spears. Her last ditch effort to get to Jess before being apprehended had almost gotten Chief of Police Dan Burnett killed. The memory quaked through Jess even now.

Dan was far more than Birmingham's highest-ranking cop. He was the man Jess loved and the father of the child she carried. Thankfully, he was released from the hospital yesterday. Cracked ribs, a mild concussion, and stitches where a bullet grazed his forehead weren't so bad considering he could have been killed during his bold move to stop Amanda. At gunpoint, he'd crashed his SUV, totaling the vehicle, rather than taking her to Jess. Each time she thought about how the encounter between Dan and Amanda might have ended, Jess's heart squeezed.

Amanda remained hospitalized for the ongoing psychiatric evaluation. How much of her story was truth and how much was fiction continued to be an unknown variable.

The cell chimed again before Jess's probing fingers curled around it and pulled it from the bottomless pit she badly needed to organize. The name displayed on the screen chilled her blood. *Tormenter.* One swipe and Eric Spears's words filled the text box, prompting a blast of fury in her hot enough to burn away the chill.

Yet another man who let you down, Jess. Just like your father.

Jess turned all the way around, scouring the tree line for the other reality she had been forced to face in recent weeks. Every minute of every day someone was out there watching her and reporting to Spears.

"Coward."

Let them watch.

One by one, they were going down.

CHAPTER TWO

Senator Robert Baron's historic home sat on more than seven acres of prime real estate with breathtaking views on all sides. The house was a sprawling twenty thousand square feet. The backyard, complete with vibrant fountains and lush landscape, would put to shame the gardens surrounding a luxurious resort hotel.

The lavish presentation was a little overwhelming, beautiful, but overwhelming. Jess couldn't see herself in a home this imposing. Cradling her sparkling water, she glanced up at the man at her side and wondered if this was his notion of the ideal home he wanted one day. His home on Dunbrooke—the one he'd lost to the fire—hadn't been quite so ostentatious. Jess had spent a great deal of time at Dan's home before the fire. She'd grown comfortable in that house with him. The truth was she could be comfortable anywhere as long as he was there.

Dan leaned her way and murmured, "I know that look."

The sound of his voice sent a familiar and sweet little shiver through her. Jess had been in love with Dan Burnett for more than two decades and still his voice, simply looking at him, undid her in a way she'd never been able to restrain.

"I beg your pardon," she murmured back, opting not to meet his gaze. She'd always had a weak spot for those blue eyes of his, too. The square jaw and those cute dimples were pretty amazing as well.

"You're thinking," he went on, somehow seeming closer than before, "how sorry you feel for Sylvia and Nina having grown up in such a formal atmosphere. Trust me, it's not like that and wasn't when they were kids. The Barons enjoy their home. They *live* in it, Jess, in every sense of the word."

Dan would certainly know from experience. Nina, Sylvia's younger sister, was his second wife. During law school, Nina had been diagnosed with a serious mental illness. Still, she graduated at the top of her class and went on to have a very successful law practice. Shortly after her brief marriage to Dan eleven years ago, she stopped taking her meds and the happily ever after ended. Since her illness had been kept a secret and with his work schedule in the department, he hadn't recognized the critical symptoms until it was too late. Delusional, paranoid and in an utter state of panic, Nina had tried to shoot Dan with his own weapon. Afterward she retreated inside herself, and that was where she'd stayed since, leaving little hope of ever understanding why she suddenly considered him a threat.

"The lack of hominess might have crossed my mind," Jess admitted quietly, not wanting to be overheard. There were at least two hundred people mingling about the house and gardens. This was no simple family barbecue. The who's who of Birmingham was here. "Actually," she teased, "I was counting all your exes."

Jess surveyed the crowd looking for the chic cream-colored dress Gina Coleman was wearing. They'd spoken briefly when Jess first arrived. "You could have your own reality show with all these gorgeous women."

Gina, Birmingham's award-winning TV news journalist, and Dan had once enjoyed a sort of friends with benefits relationship that ended with Jess's return. Then there was Annette Denton, Dan's third and most recent ex-wife. Jess spotted the lovely brunette in her dazzling white dress huddled with a handsome man who was not her current and soon-to-be ex-husband. *Interesting.* The ex Jess really wanted to meet wasn't in attendance. Meredith Dority, his first wife, had recently aligned with the mayor in his plot to remove Dan as chief of police. The move was completely out of character based on what Dan had told Jess about his first wife—another mystery Jess wanted desperately to solve.

"Trust me, if I had a reality show," he whispered against her ear, "you would be the star."

Jess turned her face up to his to see the grin she heard in his voice. The small bandage on his forehead made her heart ache. "What I was really thinking is how beautiful Nina looks and how sad it is that the doctors here don't seem to be able to help her."

Nina Baron sat in a comfortable chair. Like Sylvia, Nina was dressed to the nines. An equally well-dressed woman stood beside Nina. The nurse, Jess had learned when Dan had made the introductions. Nina hadn't so much as blinked at either of them.

The senator would no doubt give all of this and more to have his daughter back. Jess couldn't imagine the pain of having a child with a debilitating illness. Instinctively, her hand went to her belly. Being pregnant made her more aware than ever of that fear. She hoped she and Dan never had to know that anguish.

"They're moving Nina to the New York facility next week." His voice was somber now. "It won't be easy on the family."

"Or the patient," Jess said, thinking aloud. New York was a long way from Alabama. Nina's father was still looking for the miracle that would bring his little girl back. When did a parent give up on finding a miracle for their child, no matter the age? Never, she surmised. Being a parent was hard work with plenty of difficult decisions.

She thought of Maddie Brownfield, the little girl whose mother was a cold-blooded killer. Jess had dropped by to check on her yesterday. She'd intended to visit her again today, but another murder investigation had gotten in the way. The child's entire future hung in the balance. The possibility that she would end up in foster care as Jess and Lily had was more than a little troubling, it was unacceptable.

The day Jess and her sister had been told about their parents' accident was the last day she recalled any sort of childhood normalcy. As soon as Helen and Lee Harris died, Jess and Lil had been thrust into chaos—first with their unreliable aunt and then into foster care.

"Okay, we need to mingle." Dan placed his hand at the small of her back. "You're supposed to be relaxing right now."

The man knew her too well. What she really wanted was to work. Each minute she wasted was another that Spears gained. How could she relax and pretend he wasn't out there plotting his next move? Selecting his next victim? Lately, her every case revolved around him…and *her*.

"I'm trying." She gave Dan a hopeful smile. Relaxing was good for the baby. She knew this, she simply needed to find a way to put that knowledge into practice.

"Come with me." He ushered her forward. "The Senator will not be happy if I don't introduce the two of you. He's mentioned more than once that he wanted to meet you."

"Sure." Jess kept her smile in place when what she really wanted to do was wince. There had been no time to change after work before coming here.

The red skirt with its matching belted jacket was the closest thing to dress up apparel she owned at the moment anyway. She'd spritzed on a hint of her favorite perfume just to make sure the odor of coagulated blood wasn't lingering, then she'd freshened her mascara and lip gloss and called it good enough.

A number of couples, including Mayor Joseph Pratt and his wife, surrounded Senator Robert Baron. Jess stifled a groan. Pratt's recent efforts to undermine Dan's reputation and worse made her furious. Despite the timing, she doubted the mayor's machinations could be blamed on Spears. Mayor Joseph Pratt had his own malicious agenda.

To her immense relief, Pratt and his wife drifted away from the group as Jess and Dan approached. Apparently, he wasn't happy to see them either. Senator Baron, on the other hand, seemed delighted. He immediately shifted his attention to the two of them. Baron was an attractive man nearing seventy. Tall and fit, his gray hair made him look distinguished rather than old.

"Dan." The Senator thrust out his hand. "I was just bragging about the incredible job you continue to do despite the recent pressures we're all hearing about in the news."

"Thank you, sir." Dan shook the older man's outstretched hand. "I wanted to introduce you to a very special lady."

Baron grinned. "No need for an introduction. I've already heard all about this lady from Sylvia."

Jess offered her hand. "It's a pleasure to meet you, Senator."

He gave her hand a firm shake. "The pleasure is mine, Jess. Dan is a very lucky man to have you on his team."

"I remind him of that every day," Jess assured him.

Senator Baron's hearty laughter made her smile. Maybe her old friend Buddy Corlew was wrong. She might have grown up on the other side of the tracks from these wealthy people, but she belonged here, Jess decided, as surely as anyone else in attendance.

Dan's parents appeared and the conversation shifted to fundraising projects.

"This could go on all night." Katherine Burnett patted Jess's arm. "You look very nice, dear. How are you feeling?"

Wow, a compliment that didn't involve being compared to a hunting dog. Hopefully, Dan's mother had decided to accept her. "Thank you. I'm feeling well."

"Have you and Dan had time to look for a new home?"

They really did need to get around to finding one. "Not yet, but house hunting is definitely on our agenda."

"I keep an eye on all the best properties." Katherine gave a knowing nod. "I'd love to help."

Jess almost changed the subject. The words were on the tip of her tongue, then she reminded herself that this woman, despite all the times she had treated

Jess badly, would be her child's grandmother. She was Dan's mother. Why fight the inevitable? "Any suggestions you have would be appreciated. Finding time in our schedules lately has been impossible."

For about twenty-five years, Katherine Burnett had not considered Jess good enough for her son, and still the relief that shone in her eyes at hearing a positive response touched Jess.

"I'll speak to my realtor tomorrow and send you and Dan a list of properties," Katherine promised.

"Thank you, Katherine. That sounds like a good starting place."

"Harris!" Sylvia Baron sidled up and took Jess by the arm. "Forgive me," she announced unrepentantly to the small group, "but I need to steal Harris away for a moment."

With a chorus of assurances echoing behind them, Sylvia ushered Jess in the direction of the mansion's grand rear entrance.

"We have to talk, Harris."

"You have my undivided attention." Jess plucked an hors d'oeuvre from a passing platter. The bacon wrapped date with a touch of Parmesan was scrumptious.

Sylvia greeted more guests and introduced Jess each time before ushering her into a study where a large desk flanked by comfortable wingbacks sat in front of floor to ceiling bookshelves.

Once the door was closed, Sylvia collapsed against it. "Thank God. This annual event grows bigger each year."

"Your father has many friends." Jess sipped her sparkling water, wishing she had grabbed two of those bacon wrapped thingies.

"Along with a few enemies." The ME quirked an eyebrow. "Daddy taught me long ago to keep my friends close and my enemies closer."

"He's a smart man."

Sylvia frowned, looked Jess up and down. "Weren't you wearing *that* at the homicide scene this morning?"

Jess decided not to mention that she felt inordinately lucky that it even still fit. "There was no time to change. Besides, I've been too busy for any shopping."

"Too busy to shop?" Sylvia pressed a hand to her chest. "Be still my heart." She pushed away from the door and headed to the liquor cabinet. "I wasn't going to tell you about this find until tomorrow morning."

"What find?" When Sylvia left the chapel, she'd insisted she couldn't start the autopsy on the reverend before tomorrow. Understandable. Jess's cases weren't the only ones that needed the attention of the coroner's office. After leaving the chapel this morning, Jess and Hayes had checked in at the scene in Scottsboro while Harper, Lori, and Cook worked on tracking down the family and friends of the reverend. Not an easy task with this being a holiday weekend. Most folks were either trying to fit in one final escape before summer ended or were off to a big family gathering not unlike this one.

In the end, they'd learned no earth shattering revelations about the reverend and nothing new on Amanda Brownfield. Not a single member of the Joint Task Force had anything new or otherwise on Spears.

They needed a significant break. *Soon.*

"I couldn't stand the suspense." Sylvia had a long drink from her Scotch. "I started the preliminary on Henshaw."

Her interest overriding all else, Jess set her glass aside and joined the ME at the bar. "You can't have any tox screen results." The drug ketamine was a classic Spears choice, and at least one of his followers had used Curare to immobilize victims.

Sylvia shook her head. "No tox results yet." She shrugged her silk clad shoulders. "I don't know. Maybe I've watched too many movies, but I couldn't stop wondering. So I worked on dissolving the glue holding his palms together to see if there was anything there, and then I removed the sutures from his lips."

Having spent more than a decade as a profiler for the Bureau, Jess understood the sutured lips were likely about silence or secrets. "What'd you find?" Clearly, her friend had found something.

"A key. Under his tongue."

"I need to see that key." Jess wasn't sure the senator would like his daughter disappearing on him, but whatever new message Spears was sending, she needed to find it as quickly as possible.

"I expected that reaction." Sylvia went to the desk and retrieved her cell. "I snapped a pic. I don't think it's a safety deposit box key. It's definitely not a house or car key."

Jess studied the image of the key. Bow on the end. Shank an inch or so long. The single bit suggested an old key or a reproduction of an old one. Every item she'd inspected at the Brownfield house ticked off in her brain, but there was nothing the key would fit. "This looks more like one you'd find in a vintage desk or trunk."

"That's my thinking. I'll send the photo to you." Sylvia tapped the screen a few times before setting her phone aside. "Whatever it is," she said, her gaze shifting to Jess, "it was important enough that Spears murdered a man to deliver it to you. We both know that's what he's been doing for the past ten or so bodies. He's sending you messages."

As if Jess needed a reminder of that cold, hard fact. "Good work, Sylvia."

Sylvia gave her a nod. "I want you to find this sick bastard."

The sooner the better.

8:10 P.M.

The car stopped and Jess opened her eyes. It wasn't that late but she was exhausted. According to her sister and her obstetrician, feeling physically drained all the time happened in the first trimester and was nothing to be concerned about. It would subside as she moved beyond week twelve. Jess looked forward to reaching that milestone.

"Where are we?" She peered through the glass, trying to identify the neighborhood. They certainly weren't on Conroy Road at her garage apartment—the one Dan shared with her for now.

He held up a key. "I want to show you a house."

She didn't see a For Sale sign. "Did you make a final decision on buying rather than building?" That was one decision she preferred to leave up to him. He'd probably told her already and she'd forgotten. Apparently, she was already suffering from the *momnesia* her sister had warned her about.

"It takes time to build a house, Jess," he reminded her gently. "I don't want us living over some old guy's garage when the baby comes."

He had a valid point there. She hadn't paid any attention to what direction he'd driven. "Where are we?"

"A couple of streets over from Dunbrooke. A friend called to tell me about the listing before it goes on the market. Properties go fast around here."

She was so ready for a long hot shower and bed, but Dan sounded as if this meant a lot to him. "We're lucky to get a heads up. Let's check it out."

Before she'd opened the door of the sedan he'd rented, Dan was at her side. On the street, the BPD cruiser that followed her everywhere she went these days waited.

"Your realtor friend might want to warn the neighbors about us," she teased.

Dan chuckled. "If we keep making the news, we may have to change our names."

The light-hearted banter was a welcome reprieve from their usual serious conversations about work and Spears. If they were a normal couple, they might share moments like this every day.

Would they ever be normal? Wishful thinking. The life of a cop rarely fit neatly into the *normal* category.

The house was larger than the one on Dunbrooke had been. Discreet landscape lighting showcased the pristine red brick home. Dan inserted the key into the lock, opened the door, and flipped on the lights. A few clicks on the keypad near the door and the beeping of the security system went silent.

Jess surveyed the entry hall. Wood floors. High ceilings. Heavy crown molding. "This is nice."

"Four bedrooms," he said as he showed her into a large great room. "Five baths. Extra large lot. All the amenities we could ever want."

Jess thought of her ranch style home in Virginia she'd recently sold. At some point, she had to take a trip up there for the closing. This house was larger than the one she'd owned and more luxurious, but not too grand. "Really nice."

Lil would love it. Her sister was a decorating addict. She never missed the annual Christmas tour of historic homes in Birmingham. Her idea of a nice Sunday drive included dropping by realtor-hosted open houses. Jess had always been too absorbed in one case or the other to care about where she laid her head at night. Her desk worked fine when needed. Things were different now. She, Dan, and the baby needed a real home. A *Burnett* home, she mused.

"Wait until you see this." He guided her into the kitchen. "Now this is a family kitchen."

"Bigger than the one you had, that's for sure." Top of the line appliances and cabinets filled the generously sized room.

Dan took her by the hands and pulled her close. "A lot of things are going to change, Jess. Our child will need us home at a decent hour with quality time to share."

A couple of elephants suddenly settled on her chest. How on earth would they manage to take care of this child? Right now—at this very moment—they needed a house, a new vehicle for Dan, an outright miracle to keep him from losing his job, and someone to teach her how to spend quality time somewhere besides at work.

Oh, and she couldn't forget the serial killer obsessed with her.

"This house is great." She chewed her lower lip for a second as she took in the gorgeous details of the room and wished the pressure in her chest would go away. "I'm a terrible cook, Dan. You know that. We'd starve if you didn't cook or we didn't order take out. I don't know how to leave work on time. I'm a woman and I rarely remember to shop."

Dan smiled at her and the pressure eased. He pulled her into his arms and held her close. "We'll figure all this out, Jess. You don't need to worry.

We're a team. We'll learn the ropes of how to be good parents together."

She breathed a little easier. He was right. They would work out all the details. There was nothing to worry about.

Except Eric Spears.

CHAPTER THREE

"I'll check in with Harper and see how it's going in Irondale." Detective Lori Wells's words, though spoken softly, seemed to echo in the long sterile corridor.

The notion that the patient would open up more with only Jess in the room was an excuse. The true motive for the decision to interview Amanda Brownfield alone was one Jess had no desire to analyze or to share, not even with Lori, a good detective as well as a good friend. Jess was grateful she seemed to understand. Whatever came out of Amanda's mouth, Jess wanted to hear it first. The need was a defense mechanism that proved even career cops were human.

"After you speak to Harper," Jess went on, "talk to Cook and find out what's going on in Scottsboro." She needed to be in three places at once today. "We'll head there after we drop by the coroner's office."

Lori said something in response, but the words didn't register. Jess was focused once more on the patient beyond the glass. Amanda was confined to her bed. Wrist and ankle restraints, along with a waist shackle warned all who entered the room she was dangerous. In addition to the security of the psychiatric unit, a BPD uniform stood guard outside her room twenty-four/seven.

How had Spears found this woman? If this connection to Jess through her father was one he had somehow staged, he'd outdone himself. On the other hand, if this woman truly was her half sister, how had Spears discovered that decades old secret?

Amanda was about the same height as Jess, a little heavier with the same brown eyes. She had lightened her hair to try to match the blond color Jess had inherited from her mother. No matter the steps she took, she wasn't anything like Jess. Amanda Brownfield was a psychopathic serial killer who needed to cause harm for pleasure. Nothing she said or did could be trusted. Her singular goal in life was achieving her own perverted desire. She suffered from delusions of grandeur and sexual fantasies involving other serial killers. Not a pretty picture.

Being born into a multi-generational family of killers, Amanda had learned the art of killing at a very early age. Killing appeared to be a ritual passed down through several generations. Whether the environment in which she was raised or the genes she inherited or a combination of both had created the psychotic criminal she was today, Jess couldn't say. What she did know was that Amanda had murdered her own mother and her boyfriend as well as dumped her daughter to dedicate herself fully to doing Spears's bidding. Amanda Brownfield evidently had found the answer to her twisted fantasies in Eric Spears.

Like the followers before her, Matthew Reed, Richard Ellis, Fergus Cagle aka the Man in the Moon and countless others, she obeyed Spears's every command.

All Jess wanted from her was a way to reach Spears.

She opened the door and entered the stark room that looked exactly like the other seventeen in the unit.

"Well if it isn't my big sister." Amanda smiled, a duplicitous expression. "Did you bring me flowers? I hear lilies are your favorite."

"Don't you have anything original to say, Ms. Brownfield?" Jess stopped at the foot of her bed and blatantly studied the woman. "This regurgitating of what Spears spouts has become increasingly tedious."

Amanda snorted. "Don't be so formal, sis. Call me Amanda. Have you picked a name for your baby? You could name her after me, if it's a girl. I'm sure Dan would like that. He's cute in an uptight sort of way."

Jess stemmed the anger that stirred inside her, recognizing that was Amanda's goal. "Why don't we talk about all those people you and your grandfather murdered, Amanda? The more you cooperate, the better this will go for you."

Her gaze narrowed. "You're forgetting our daddy. He was a part of the family fun, too." Her eyebrows drew together in puzzlement. "Do you have to fight the urge to kill, Jess? I mean, it runs in our blood. You must feel it. It's like a fire. Not even sex gives me that kind of rush."

It took every ounce of strength Jess possessed to ignore her claims. One way or another, she intended to keep this interview focused on finding Spears. "Beyond the remains we've found, I have no interest in your past, Amanda, real or imagined. Let's concentrate on the present and how we can get you out of this place."

A wary interest sparked in her gaze. "You can't do that," she challenged. "They're never going to let me out." To punctuate her words, she tested the strength of her restraints, the pain of doing so clouding her face. "They'll label me crazy and I'll chill out in some fancy hospital until I get old and die. My life is already over and we both know it."

"I hate to disappoint you, Amanda, but I've spoken with the DA. He doesn't intend to allow you to get off that easily."

"Whatever." Amanda stared at the ceiling. "Like I said, you don't have the power to get me out of here."

"You'd be surprised what I can do." Jess removed a pad and pencil from her bag before settling it on the floor. "I have very important contacts in the Federal Bureau of Investigation. You already know the chief of police is in love with me. He'll do whatever I ask. What he says carries a lot of influence around here."

Still visibly suspicious, Amanda took the bait. "What would I have to do?"

"You have to prove you're willing to cooperate. Tell me more about how you came to be involved with Spears and how you contact him. Whatever you can give me might help our investigation. And it'll help you, Amanda." Jess moved up to the side of the bed. "Sheriff Foster has already handed jurisdiction over to us. I'm the only person in a position to help you."

Another of those malicious smiles spread across Amanda's face. "Maybe Eric will get me out. He's far more brilliant than all you cops put together."

"But he isn't here, Amanda. I am." Jess paused to allow that reality to sink in. "Let me explain how Eric works. So far, everyone who helps him ends up dead. Do you really believe you'll be the exception?"

Hesitation. Jess was making progress.

"I'm not saying I believe you," Amanda made a noncommittal face, "but there are things I could tell you. Like how I saw two women in glass boxes at his house."

Anticipation fired through Jess. Could Amanda have seen Rory Stinnett and Monica Atmore? Eric Spears made a production of dumping the bodies of his victims as part of his usual MO. Since their bodies hadn't turned up, there was reason to believe the women were still alive. *We're waiting for you, Jess.*

"I'm not sure what women you mean." Jess shrugged. "Can you tell me their names?"

"You know, the two women who've been all over the news." Amanda rolled her eyes. "I don't remember their names."

Jess retrieved a copy of the updated missing persons flyer from her bag. "Are these the women you saw?"

"The first two but not the other one. I already told you I've never seen her before."

"Were the women alive? Can you describe their condition and the way they were being held?" Jess dared to hope.

"They looked fine to me." Amanda shrugged her uninjured shoulder. "He has them in glass cages in a room that's kind of like a science lab or something. He's saving them for when you get there. I told you before, this is all about you, Jess."

"I guess I was wrong about you, Amanda." Jess put the pencil and paper as well as the flyer away. "Looks like you're the first."

The wariness was back in Amanda's dark eyes. "First what?"

"No other woman has been with Eric the way you have and lived to tell about it." Jess reached out, smoothed a wisp of hair from Amanda's cheek. "I'm certain he went to great lengths to find you. I see now that you are obviously very important to him."

"Told you." Amanda looked away a moment. "As soon as he figured out we had the same daddy, he started looking for me. I already knew who he was. I'd been following the stuff about the Player on that investigation channel even before I knew his real name. Then one day he called me. We talked like we'd known each other forever. He already knew all about me and you and our daddy."

Jess restrained the urge to shake the whole truth out of the woman. "What kinds of things does he know?"

Amanda laughed. "Everything, Jess. He knows more about you than you do. I didn't pay attention to most of it. I just wanted to hear his voice. It was like talking to a rock star only better."

"He sure never called me." Jess put her hand to her chest in feigned wonder. "Were you terrified?"

"I was so excited," Amanda lifted her head from the pillow to draw closer to Jess, "I came just talking to him."

Jess resisted the urge to flinch. "His voice is very intense. I spoke with him in person once, you know."

Amanda's expression turned smug. "I've talked to him lots of times."

Jess made a dismissive sound. "I knew him first."

"I doubt it. He called me on Valentine's Day, almost seven months ago."

"He made you wait seven whole months before you were…together?" Jess countered. "That's a really long time."

"Some things are worth waiting for."

"How often did he call you?"

"He mailed me a new phone every week so we could talk, then I removed the battery and threw the old one in the river just like he told me to."

"What did you talk about?"

"You, mostly." She gave Jess a knowing look. "I helped him find out all kinds of things about you and our daddy until my stupid mother found out why I was asking so many questions."

"I wish I knew more about him." Jess sighed. "No one knows where he lives. You probably didn't notice the postmark of the packages with the phones?"

"They came from all over the place. California. New York. Texas." Amanda laughed. "He's been everywhere."

Jess braced her forearms on the bedrail and pretended to relax. "I guess I'll have to wait until we're together the way you two were before I know more."

Amanda didn't speak again for twelve infinite seconds. Each one detonated in Jess's head like a carefully choreographed series of explosions.

"You said you could help me get out of here."

"First, you have to help me. Did you ever speak to any of his friends?"

"Only the one who picked me up and he didn't say a whole lot."

"We can start there." Amanda had given Jess nothing when she'd asked similar questions on Friday night and then again yesterday. After being shackled to a bed for better than forty-eight hours, maybe she was ready to talk now. "Let's go through the steps from the moment the man wearing the mask picked you up. Tell me everything you saw, heard, touched, or smelled until you laid eyes on Spears."

"He picked me up at the Oasis." Amanda sent a pointed look at Jess. "I couldn't exactly go home."

By then they were already unearthing remains at the family farm. "Were you waiting outside the club?" Jess prompted.

"I was at the bar. I know where the manager keeps his spare key. He doesn't know I know it, but that's what happens when dumbasses are in charge. Anyway, I went inside and had a couple of drinks. You know, to brace myself. Meeting Eric Spears for the first time was a big deal."

"I know what you mean." Jess had been there, done that, for entirely different reasons, of course. "So the driver wore a mask into the bar?"

Amanda started to shrug then flinched. "Sure. Didn't matter. The club was closed so no one was there except me. The dude came in, told me to put on the blindfold he tossed at me, and then he led me outside."

"How tall would you say this masked man was? What kind of mask and clothes did he wear? What color hair? Was he Caucasian?"

"He wore a ski mask. Kind of tall, maybe six feet. Dark hair. White guy, I'm pretty sure. His clothes were black. You know, like Joaquin Phoenix when he played Johnny Cash. Black shirt and black pants."

Jess's pulse bumped into a faster rhythm. If the club had video surveillance outside, they might be able to pick something up on the vehicle. "You went outside and then what happened?"

"He picked me up and put me in the trunk."

"Did the trunk smell new? Used? Think hard, Amanda."

"Smelled like a new car. And that guy wore cologne. Something expensive and sexy. Made me horny."

"How long did it take to arrive at Spears's house? Long enough for your muscles to feel cramped? Did you need to use the bathroom by the time you arrived?"

Amanda considered the questions. "By the time he stopped, I needed to pee real bad from the bourbon and cokes and I was feeling cramped up for sure. I cussed him out for keeping me in the trunk so long."

"Did you hear any traffic sounds? Was the road smooth or bumpy?"

"Road had a few bumps. There was traffic at first, and then it got quiet like we'd left town."

Given those details, Jess estimated Amanda was in the trunk for an hour and a half or more. The alcohol would have had time to metabolize to an extent and have its diuretic effect on the bladder. Ninety minutes or so was certainly long enough for her muscles to have grown stiff.

"What did you see, hear or smell once you were out of the trunk?"

Amanda shook her head. "I didn't smell anything different. It was quiet." She frowned. "I might've heard a dog before he hustled me into the house. So, when are you getting me out of here? Did you tell Lil about me?" Accusation clouded her gaze. "I bet you didn't. You don't want anyone to know, do you?"

"Let's focus on what we have to do to get you out of here right now. The rest can wait. Did you have dinner with Spears? Did he look like you thought he would?"

"I didn't have food on my mind at the time." She breathed a little laugh. "I'd seen his pictures on the news, but he looked even better in person."

"How can you be sure it was really him?" It wouldn't be the first time a follower had gone to great lengths to look like Eric Spears.

"Oh, it was him, I know for a fact."

"How do you know for a fact, Amanda?"

She made an impatient sound. "Don't you want to know about our daddy?" She grinned. "I used to hide in my momma's closet so I could watch them have sex."

"How old were you?" Jess demanded in spite of herself. She needed to keep this interview on Spears. Dammit.

"My momma loved him to the moon and back," Amanda continued, ignoring Jess completely. "It made my granddaddy crazy. When he caught them in bed together the first time, our daddy was scared to death. That's when he had to start doing whatever granddaddy told him or end up buried in the yard like all the others. Back then my granddaddy had lots of friends who came over, but our daddy was the only one my momma ever wanted."

"Did your grandfather's friends live in Scottsboro?" All Jess needed was one living witness who knew the Brownfield family's story. And her father. As desperately as she wanted to pretend this wasn't personal, it was. Dammit, it was.

"Most of them. After he died, my momma run them all off. She said she wanted no part of that mess."

"How can you remember that? You were what? Four years old when—" Jess clamped her mouth shut.

"When our daddy died?" Amanda finished for her. "My momma told me the stories when I was older. She wanted me to understand why daddy did bad things so I wouldn't hate him the way she hated her daddy." Amanda laughed. "She didn't understand I was totally like my granddaddy. I love doing bad things." She writhed beneath the thin sheet as if thinking about it made her restless. "You might, too, Jess, if you ever tried it."

Jess refused to let the woman's words get to her. "Are you sure there isn't anything else you remember about where you met Spears? If we could rescue those women, the Bureau would consider that quite a heroic deed. It could make all the difference, Amanda." Not that Jess was in any position to offer deals.

"I can't believe you haven't figured this out already, sis. He's somewhere in Birmingham. Close, *really* close." Amanda exhaled a big dramatic sigh. "Doesn't really matter where he is though. You could be standing right beside him and you wouldn't be able to save those women."

Worry gnawed at Jess. "Why not?"

Amanda laughed softly. "You can't stop him, Jess. All you can do is watch the innocent lives taken until your time comes. That's the way this game works. He always finishes the game."

"I thought you were going to help me, Amanda."

Amanda shook her head. "I can't help you. No one can."

The sound of Jess's cell shattered the tension. She stepped back and reached for it. The phone number wasn't one she recognized. "Harris."

"Chief Harris, this is Sheriff Foster over in Jackson County."

Jess took a breath. "You have something new?"

"I'm not exactly sure," Foster went on. "To tell you the truth, it's downright strange."

Jess decided against reminding him that there was a farm with somewhere in the neighborhood of forty homicide victims buried on it in his county. What could be stranger than that?

"Sometime last night a car went off the road near the old Comer Bridge over on Route 35," Foster explained. "You know the one where your folks had their accident. Anyway, a fisherman found it this morning. We're still looking for the driver or any passenger. So far we haven't found a soul."

A chill settled in her bones. "I take it you've found something though." Jess didn't use his name or rank. The less Amanda knew the better.

"Well, yes, ma'am, we did. Oddest thing. And that's saying something considering what we found last week."

Jess's point exactly.

"There was a note in the car. It was all sealed up in a plastic bag and taped to the dash. The note was addressed to you, Chief."

Any chance of drawing in a reasonable breath deserted her.

"I'll read it to you," Foster went on. "*This is where it began, Jess, and this is where it will end.*"

"I'm on my way." She severed the connection and told herself to breathe.

"Did something happen?"

Ignoring the question, Jess readied to go. "I'll be back soon, Amanda. If you remember anything, tell the officer on duty you need to speak with me. That's the only way I can help you."

"Something did happen!"

Jess didn't look back.

"He's getting closer, Jessie Lee!"

The words followed her out the door.

CHAPTER FOUR

For such a small town, the Friendly City had at least three hungry reporters giving the uniforms at the blockade on Route 35 a hard time. Jess kept her face turned away from the reporters. If anyone recognized her, the minor nuisance of a trio of local reporters would turn into an all-out circus. The scene at the Brownfield farm required a six-man team on duty around the clock to keep the newshounds and curiosity seekers off the property.

Hayes was at the Oasis with the manager reviewing the video recordings from last Friday. The only cameras were in the parking lot, which was better than nothing, and might provide the license plate number of the car the masked man had been driving. They could definitely use a good lead.

Lori braked and flashed her badge for the officer holding back traffic. He waved them through. En route, Jess had spent some time on Google learning all she could about the bridge and the number of accidents that occurred on or near it every year.

42

The historic bridge was scheduled for demolition next year. Alongside the nearly century old steel structure, a new, state of the art bridge spanned the Tennessee River. Local preservationists were working hard to prevent the tearing down of yet another piece of history. Jess stared at the looming web of steel. It looked eerie and unsafe to her, but then she was far from objective. Her parents had died in the water beneath that bridge.

What the hell was Spears up to now?

Jess had called Gant and given him the new information Amanda had passed along, whether it was reliable or not. Gant didn't share an opinion one way or the other with her. She didn't hold it against him since she hadn't shared with him Amanda's claim that she was Jess's half sister. A true team player would have done so, Jess supposed. Things had been like that between her and Gant for a while.

Gant was probably calling Chief Black right now. Harold Black was deputy chief over the BPD's Crimes Against Persons Division. He was BPD's representative on the Spears Joint Task Force. Technically, Jess should have called him first, but she hadn't done that either.

From the beginning, Black had made it clear he didn't like her. In part, she supposed, his decision had been based on an outsider coming in and taking a prized opportunity for promotion within the department. Jess understood those feelings. What she couldn't understand was his seeming determination to treat Dan as a person of interest in the case of a missing cop, the head of the Gang Task Force. Black and Dan went way back. He should have Dan's back.

Dan didn't agree with Jess on that one. He saw what Black was doing as nothing more than his job. Time would tell if he was the man Dan thought him to be. For Dan's sake, Jess hoped he was.

Lori parked her Mustang behind a Jackson County deputy's cruiser. Jess surveyed the cluster of official vehicles at the bottom of the ravine that leveled off as it reached the riverbank. From the looks of the aftermath, the car had plowed down the ravine and disappeared into the murky depths of the water.

"If there was no one in the car," Lori speculated, "someone must have rigged the accelerator to keep the vehicle going when it left the shoulder of the road."

She'd read Jess's mind. Once the vehicle left the road, it plunged some twenty or more feet down a steep incline. "And it just kept going," Jess agreed. The ground leveled off for maybe ten yards before reaching the river.

Her attention returned to the bridge. Jess wasn't clear on the precise location where her parents' vehicle had left the bridge and entered the water, but she knew it was closer to this side of the river than to the other. The railing had required repair after their car crashed through it. She remembered the officer who'd spoken to her Aunt Wanda after the funeral saying as much. He had suggested that

Jess's father had been traveling at an inordinately high rate of speed.

Why would a man with his wife in the car and two children at home counting on him be so careless?

Why was it she could only remember snippets of that time? She'd never really thought about it until now, but her memory of the first ten years of her life was vague and scattered.

Emerging from the Mustang, Jess cleared the disturbing thoughts from her mind. She glanced at her feet and wished she'd had the presence of mind to start packing sneakers for this sort of expedition. She and Lori had talked about it before. Had that been two or three cases ago? Lately, the passage of time seemed more accurately measured by the number of murders than the days and weeks on the calendar.

"You're going to be very glad I'm your ride today."

"Have you ever heard me complain?" Jess shut the car door and adjusted her sunglasses. "Besides, no one else has a sporty red car."

"I mean," Lori popped the trunk, "you'll be glad because I remembered to pack sneakers."

"I wish I could say the same." Jess carried so much in this bag now the prospect of adding a pair of sneakers had her shoulders aching.

Lori held up two pairs of sneakers like trophies. "I've got you covered, Chief."

Jess could have hugged her. "You're a lifesaver."

"Be sure to remember that when evaluations come around." Lori tossed her a pair of the sneakers.

Two minutes later, they both sported Skechers Trail running shoes in a sleek black with neon pink trim. Didn't go too well with Jess's tangerine-colored suit any more than they did with Lori's rust-colored trousers and matching summer jacket, but Jess wasn't complaining. The sneakers would make trudging up and down the grassy slope more comfortable and far less hazardous than the high heeled Mary Janes she loved.

A woman was never too old to adapt.

Descending the ravine while avoiding the obvious path the vehicle had taken proved on the precarious side even with the proper footwear. Sheriff Foster and two of his deputies stood near the silver sedan, which had been dragged from the river. Foster broke away from the group and met Jess a few yards from the vehicle.

"We decided not to have the car towed until you got here." He gave Jess a nod then another for Lori. "Chief Gleason and I talked about this and he prefers we handle anything related to this case even if it happens inside Scottsboro's city limits."

"I appreciate that, Sheriff. Be sure to thank Chief Gleason for me." Jess shifted her attention to the car. "Have you identified the owner?"

"We're working on it. The owner listed in the database claims he sold the car months ago, but the new owner never registered it. We're still trying to track the new owner down."

"Did you turn the note into evidence already?"

"I figured you'd want to see it first, too."

"I owe you one, Sheriff."

He hitched his head toward the car. "My deputy's holding on to the note for us if you'd like to have a look."

Two deputies waited by the car, an Impala. The taller of the two presented the note, protected by a clear plastic evidence bag, to Jess. She studied the plain white piece of paper with its words fashioned from letters cut out of magazines. A similar note had been pinned to Maddie's dress last week.

This is where it began, Jess, and this is where it will end.

Steadying her hand before passing the note to Lori to photograph, Jess turned her attention to the car. A quick perusal confirmed there was nothing inside except damp cloth upholstery and factory installed carpet.

"Are you continuing the search for victims?" Jess looked out over the dark water, goose bumps spilling over her skin. The Impala's windows were down, which ensured the vehicle sank faster. She doubted there would be any survivors. If Spears or one of his followers wanted the driver and anyone in the car dead, they were dead.

"Yes, ma'am," Foster assured her. "We got another team of divers coming in the next hour. We'll be at it until we're satisfied there's no one down there."

"No evidence except the tire tracks?" Jess visually traced the path the car had taken. A different angle sometimes provided a new prospective.

"We searched the area with a fine tooth comb." Foster gave a firm shake of his head. "No beer cans, liquor bottles, discharged ammo jackets, discarded food wrappers, not even a cigarette butt that wasn't already mostly disintegrated. Whoever walked away from this, assuming anyone did, they were very careful not to disturb or to leave anything."

Didn't take a genius to walk away from a scene without leaving evidence. What it did require, however, was careful planning.

Lori passed the note back to the deputy, and then gave Jess a look before glancing up to the highway. Jess followed her gaze. A man emerged from his black Ford truck. He made no move to come down the grassy hill. He simply stood there and watched.

"He's a local," Foster said with a wave to the newcomer.

"I take it you recognize him." Jess studied the man as best she could from this distance. Around six feet tall and a good hundred eighty pounds with short-cropped gray hair, his bearing said cop. The jeans, T-shirt and boots indicated he was retired or, at the very least, off duty.

"Randall McPherson," Foster explained. "ABI agent, retired."

"Does Mr. McPherson consult on your investigations?" Or possibly, he needed to speak with the sheriff for some other reason.

McPherson looked directly at Jess before he turned, climbed back into his truck, and drove away.

Perhaps he only wanted to find out what all the fuss was about.

"Jackson County was part of his territory," Foster explained. "He was buddies with the trooper who worked the accident your parents were in." The sheriff glanced out over the water. "He was new to the area back then."

"Did McPherson have a part in the investigation?" The one report Jess had read was the trooper's report. Unfortunately, the trooper was now deceased. Lori had checked for a BPD investigation related to the accident but hadn't found one. Apparently, Buddy Corlew's source had gotten that one wrong. If the BPD investigated her parents' deaths, there was no record of the case.

Foster shrugged. "Alabama Bureau of Investigation and the troopers are both part of Public Safety. Mac was pretty hands-on with his jurisdiction, you know. Anything went on down here, he wanted to know about it."

Do tell. "I'm certain men like McPherson make your citizens feel safe."

"You got it," Foster confirmed. He turned his attention back to the Impala for a moment. "We'll go ahead and make the call to the Joint Task Force on this and hand over the evidence. Let me know if I can do anything else for you, Chief."

Jess thanked the sheriff and started the climb back up to the street.

"I have McPherson's home address and phone number." As usual, Lori hadn't wasted any time preparing for the next move. "I can set up a meet."

"Let's not give him a heads up." Jess paused to fan her face once they reached the asphalt again. The temperature had to be ninety-five. "Sometimes surprise visits prove far more informative."

Lori rounded the hood of her Mustang. "Not to mention more interesting."

TUPELO PIKE, 2:15 P.M.

"The truck's here." Lori eased into the gravel drive, parking squarely behind the black Ford pickup McPherson had been driving.

The front door was open, but the screen door prevented Jess from seeing inside. Or maybe it was the darkness. There was no visible light beyond the tightly drawn shades of the windows. Maybe McPherson liked the dark. He'd worked this jurisdiction for over thirty years, eventually making Scottsboro his home. According to Foster, McPherson had made it his business to know the people and the place. How had he missed what the Brownfields were doing right under his nose?

Notification that she'd received a text had Jess digging for her phone. Why was it the darned thing always found its way to the very bottom of her bag? She read the message from Sylvia. "Dr. Baron would like us at her office before five."

Lori checked the time. "As long as we head that way by three-fifteen, I can make it happen. Gives us an hour before we need to leave."

Jess contemplated the modest home with its painted clapboard siding and shingled roof. "An hour should be plenty of time to get this guy's story." *Unless he has something to hide.*

Five seconds after she and Lori were out of the Mustang, a deep, throaty growl made the hair on the back of Jess's neck stand on end and had her calculating whether it was quicker to go for the car door or for the hood.

Jump or dive?

The German shepherd lunged off the porch.

Wishing for pepper spray, Jess held her ground. On the street behind her, a car door slammed. Her surveillance detail was coming. Completely focused on her and Lori, the dog didn't seem to notice the approaching uniform.

"Come here, boy," Lori said firmly.

The dog waited halfway between where he'd hit the ground and where they stood at the front of the Mustang. Body tense, tail high and wagging slowly, he shifted his full attention toward Lori.

"Get back in the car," she said to Jess. "I got this."

Not happening. Jess reached into her bag. She had crackers in there somewhere. The dog growled again, raising goose bumps on her skin.

"Roger! Stay!" The command boomed from inside the house.

The dog dropped into a sitting position, his attention lingering on Jess.

McPherson opened the screen door and stepped out onto the porch. "Come," he ordered.

The big dog hustled up the steps to stand next to his master.

The sound of the car door closing behind Jess signaled that her surveillance detail had returned to his cruiser.

Jess relaxed. "Roger?" she asked of the man now watching her so intently. "I would've expected something like Terminator or Killer."

"He was nothing but a pup when he wandered onto my doorstep," McPherson said, glancing down as his pet. "My wife had left me for another man. I decided I'd name the dog after that lowlife bastard. Seemed fair at the time." He ruffled the fur at the dog's nape. "A year later, my ex went off her rocker, shot the guy and herself. Old Roger turned out to be the best thing that ever happened to me. This one and the other one." He stared at Jess then, his gaze narrowing. "Why're you here?"

"I'm Deputy Chief Harris from the Birmingham Police Department. This is Detective Wells. We'd like to ask you a few questions about an old case, if you have a moment."

"I've been retired for seven years, Chief. I'm afraid I don't know anything that could help you, ladies."

"That's strange," Jess challenged before he could disappear into the house. "Sheriff Foster said nothing happened in your jurisdiction that you didn't know about. Yet, we dug up a whole slew of bodies right down the road."

McPherson's face darkened. "I've already spoken to the agent in charge at the Brownfield farm and given him my insights—for what they're worth. A good cop would know things like that before she went accusing a man of something."

"You know how it is with those Bureau boys," she shot right back. "Sometimes they don't like to share." Jess shrugged. "Personally, I prefer to hear the story straight from the source."

The determined set of his jaw as well as his tense posture warned he wasn't in the mood to chat. "The Brownfields kept to themselves. Never openly broke the law or caused any trouble until Amanda turned sixteen. I'm sure you've seen her rap sheet already. As for all those bodies, I was as surprised as the rest of the cops crawling all over that farm."

"There was an accident near the bridge—"

"I can't help you with your parents' accident either since I wasn't involved in the investigation. That was Trooper Darrell Neilson. I expect you know that already, too."

"What makes you think I'm here about my parents' accident?" Jess challenged.

"I know why you're here, Chief Harris. No need to pretend otherwise."

Foster or someone on his team had evidently already leaked the note to this guy. Great. "Whether you were the investigator or not, you must have formed some conclusions based on what Trooper Neilson told you. I understand you were friends."

Three, maybe four seconds elapsed.

"Your father was driving too fast. For whatever reason, he lost control of the car. No alcohol involved based on the blood alcohol test." McPherson shrugged. "Maybe they were fighting and he wasn't paying attention. It happens."

"Did you look at the car? Or the bodies?" That thread of tension related to her parents' deaths that never really went away, tightened as images formed to go with the words.

"You're wasting your time asking me questions. There were no witnesses. The investigation found no trouble with the car and no road conditions that would've made driving hazardous that night. It was an accident. That's what Trooper Neilson said in his report. I'm sure you've read it for yourself. If not, I suggest you do so."

With that, McPherson disappeared inside, the screen door slamming behind him.

"Well then," Jess grumbled, "I guess we won't have to keep Dr. Baron waiting after all."

Lori met her gaze over the roof of her shiny red car. "Are you letting him off the hook that easily?"

"For now."

As Lori backed out of the drive, Jess reached for her cell. "I'll let Dr. Baron know we're on our way." Before she could open her contacts list, Hayes called. Jess hit the speaker option. "I hope you have good news for me, Lieutenant. I have you on speaker. Detective Wells is with me."

"The good news is Amanda Brownfield was telling the truth."

"Go on, Lieutenant."

"A man wearing a ski mask picked her up at the club. Her description was on target."

Surely the vehicle the man was driving was on the video as well. "Did you get anything on the car?"

"That's the bad news. The driver must have noticed the security cameras because he backed all the way out of range, keeping the license plate away from the camera."

Not the news she wanted to hear. "You can see what kind of car he was driving, right?" At least that would give them something.

"Oh yeah," Hayes confirmed. "He's driving a black Infiniti."

Jess and Lori exchanged a knowing look. "Thank you, Lieutenant. We need a copy of that footage."

"Taking care of it now."

The call ended and Jess tucked her phone away.

"So our dark-haired friend is back." Lori eased into traffic on Willow Street.

"Looks that way."

Jess had first spotted the dark-haired man in the Infiniti about a month ago. He'd nudged the back bumper of her car. When she'd looked in the rearview mirror, he'd been holding a handgun aimed at her. As he'd driven away, she'd received a text from Spears. *Bang! Do you like this game so far?*

She'd spotted the dark-haired man several times after that day, watching her and delivering the occasional message from Spears, until about two weeks ago when he'd seemed to vanish.

"He's been MIA for the past couple of weeks," Lori said, echoing Jess's thought.

"I guess he's back."

"Better the devil you know."

Spears followers seemed to come out of nowhere. There was no way of recognizing those faces of evil coming at them until a message was delivered, usually with a body.

Jess might not know his name, but, as Lori pointed out, this follower she could at least see coming.

JEFFERSON COUNTY CORONER'S
OFFICE, 5:20 P.M.

"Someone wanted the good reverend to bleed out a little more slowly, but not slow enough to risk anyone finding him in time to save him."

Jess studied the slash to Gordon Henshaw's femoral artery in his left thigh. "What do you mean?"

Sylvia picked up a scalpel. "If you want the blood to flow quickly without impediment, you cut the artery at an angle so the walls can't attempt to close themselves. In this instance, your killer was very careful. He made a nice straight incision. The artery walls immediately contracted, attempting to restrict the blood flow, which slowed exsanguination by several minutes."

Anger expanded in Jess's chest. Spears made this man suffer...to send her a message. Spears was a sociopathic serial killer. Causing pain and death gave him pleasure, but this victim—this poor old man—was chosen because he was connected to her past.

Your aunt says you've been getting into fights at school. Jess remembered sitting in Preacher Gordon's office and explaining how the other kid had hit her first. She'd done exactly what her new friend, Buddy Corlew, had told her to do. Her aunt, Wanda Newsom, had hauled her all the way to Irondale to see Henshaw.

Jess blocked the sights and sounds from her childhood. With far too many questions and not nearly enough answers about her past, there was at least one she had the power to resolve. "I need DNA testing on Amanda Brownfield."

Sylvia arched an eyebrow in blatant speculation. "Do we have a comparison source?"

"We do. You can take the necessary sample now."

Sylvia held Jess's gaze for a long moment. "I see."

"How long will it take?"

"I have a friend at one of the private labs in town. With a priority rush, I could possibly have something back to you by the end of the week."

"The end of the week would be good."

If Amanda Brownfield was related to her by blood, Jess wanted to know.

CHAPTER FIVE

"State your name and rank for the record."

"Chief of Police Daniel Burnett." Dan gritted his teeth to prevent telling his old friend that everyone in the damned room knew who he was. These proceedings were unnecessary. Taking a breath, he reminded himself to relax. He'd spent too much time being prepped by his attorney, Frank Teller, to screw up right out of the gate.

Deputy Chief Harold Black, Birmingham's Crimes Against Persons Division Chief, looked over his notes before continuing. Lieutenant Kelvin Roark, Harold's second in command, sat next to him, the massive case file on the missing Captain Allen lay on the table.

This couldn't be happening.

In the seemingly endless seconds that followed as Dan was sworn in, he tried to understand how this situation had progressed to the point of spiraling out of control. Captain Ted Allen had been a good

58

cop for more than a decade. When had he stopped? More importantly, why hadn't Dan noticed?

When Harold hesitated to review his notes before moving on, Teller spoke up, "It is almost six o'clock, Chief Black. Is there some reason you are not prepared to proceed?"

"I assure you, Mr. Teller, I am ready to proceed." Harold's attention rested on his notes once more.

"Then I suggest you begin."

Teller had made it abundantly clear that Dan was to let him handle this interrogation. At the time, Dan had said something like *happy to*. Not so much now. Now he wanted to reach across the conference table and shake the hell out of Harold.

Those kinds of actions will only make you look guilty.

Dan wasn't guilty. Damn it to hell, why didn't the people who had known and trusted him for decades acknowledge this? He had a job and a life that needed his attention.

"I apologize for taking a moment." Harold looked up and offered a smile. "I needed to refresh my memory. Now. Chief Burnett, I'm going to ask you a series of questions that may seem repetitive, bear with me, please. We need to do this for the official record of this proceeding."

Dan leaned back in his chair and tried again to at least appear at ease.

"You're aware that Captain Ted Allen remains missing," Harold stated.

"Yes," Dan answered.

"As the head of the department's Gang Task Force, Captain Allen answered directly to you and met with you approximately once each week, is that correct?"

"Yes." Dan considered for a second or two the rest of what he wanted to say. "He did until about two months ago. At that time, his work required increasingly more of his attention so we often spoke by phone."

"When did you become aware of Captain Allen's work related issues with Deputy Chief Harris? For the record," Harold went on, "Chief Harris is the Division Chief of the Special Problems Unit."

Dan tensed at the mention of Jess's name. He didn't want her dragged into this any more deeply than she already was. She didn't need the stress. "I became aware of the situation during the investigation of the DeShawn Simmons' case, the final week of July." Dan still couldn't think of Jess going into a drug lord's house demanding answers without starting to sweat. She could have been killed right there under the surveillance of the Gang Task Force.

"The tension between Captain Allen and Chief Harris continued to escalate, noticeably so during the Grayson murder investigation, until he disappeared on or about August 6, is that correct?" Harold folded his hands in front of him and looked to Dan for a response.

"Yes. The Grayson case involved the murder of Lieutenant Lawrence Grayson's wife. Most of the department, as you well know, was in an uproar over

Chief Harris' decision to investigate Lieutenant Grayson and his partner, Sergeant Jack Riley."

"This investigation," Harold began, "created quite a bad feeling toward Chief Harris."

"Please rephrase your remark into the form of a question, Chief Black," Teller advised, "and identify who allegedly had a bad feeling toward Chief Harris."

"Of course. Is it true," Harold tried again, "that Chief Harris' investigation into Grayson and Riley created a bad feeling toward her within the department?"

"Chief Harris proved to be correct about the murder," Dan answered gladly. "Sergeant Riley and his wife were responsible for Mrs. Grayson's murder."

"Be that as it may, you didn't answer my question," Harold argued.

"How is any of this relevant to my client's alleged involvement in Captain Allen's disappearance?" Teller demanded. "This is becoming nothing more than a fishing expedition as well as a colossal waste of time and tax payer dollars."

Harold shifted his attention to the attorney. "Mr. Teller, we are investigating the potential homicide of one of our own. Determining the circumstances of all events leading up to Captain Allen's disappearance is crucial to ruling out the possibility that anyone in this department was involved in his disappearance."

"You mean," Dan cut in, too damned frustrated now to keep his mouth shut, "like the possibility that I was the one who made him disappear."

"Please, Dan," Teller said firmly, "wait for a new question."

Harold sighed. "I'll move on to another question. As chief of police, what did you do to control the situation between Chief Harris and Captain Allen?"

Dan searched for calm. All he had to do was answer truthfully and professionally. One step at a time, he would get through this. "I warned Captain Allen that he'd better show the proper respect to his superior. I urged Chief Harris to find a way to work with Captain Allen. That's it. I have no idea how his cell phone ended up in my trashcan. I have—"

"You've answered the question, Dan," Teller cautioned, cutting him off.

Dan ignored him. "I have no idea how Allen's wedding band came to be in my barbecue grill. But I do know a set up when I see one."

"For the record," Teller interjected, "both the trashcan and the barbecue grill were easily accessible to anyone passing on the street."

"So noted, Mr. Teller," Harold stated.

Dan didn't trust his instincts about Harold anymore. They had been friends for years, but then, so had he and the mayor. At this point, he wasn't sure who he could trust besides Jess.

"The fire at your home was ruled arson," Harold commented.

"Is that a question, Chief Black? What are you suggesting?" Teller countered.

Harold shook his head. "I'm not suggesting any-thing, sir." His attention rested on Dan once more. "I'm desperate to solve this case and clear up the confusion."

Teller stood. "Well then, until you have enough evidence to consider Chief Burnett a suspect, I would *suggest* you stop harassing him with the same questions he's already answered." He looked to Dan. "This proceeding is over."

Feeling more helpless and frustrated than he had when they started, Dan pushed out of his chair.

"Dan," Harold stood, "I hope you know I'm doing all I can to sort this out."

"I'm confident you are, Harold." There was a lot more Dan wanted to say, but he decided to be smart and do as his attorney advised this time. Jess needed him to be smart. Whatever happened with this case affected her as well as their child.

Teller waited until Harold and Roark were gone. "You did fairly well, Dan." He reached for his brief case. "Next time, remember not to give more than you're asked. Answer only the question and leave it at that. Easier said than done, I know, but it's imper-ative that you restrain the urge to give unnecessary information. You are not guilty until proven other-wise. Black is the one who has to prove his case, not you."

"That's just it." No one was listening. "There is no case against me. I had nothing to do with Allen's disappearance."

"Then we have nothing to worry about."

With that profound statement, Teller left the conference room. Dan wanted to throw something except that would probably make him look guilty, too.

He made the short journey down the hall to his office and closed the door. His secretary was already gone for the day. A stack of messages and a pile of work waited on his desk. For the first time in his career, he had no desire to tackle either.

More than anything, he wanted Jess settled. Decisions had to be made about a house and whatever else she and the baby would need in case things went more wrong than they already had. He'd made all the necessary legal arrangements in the event Spears made good on his threat that Dan wouldn't be around to raise his child. Over the years, he'd taken the trust fund he'd inherited from his grandfather and invested well. Financially, Jess and the baby would have no worries.

The headstone bearing his name that Spears had delivered elbowed its way into the other troubling thoughts. Dan knew better than to ignore the sick bastard. This very morning Spears, or one of his followers, had murdered another innocent victim, and Jess was out there trying to make sense of his moves in the hope of stopping him.

Dan closed his eyes and attempted to halt the worries mounting inside him without success. In his pocket, his cell vibrated. He snapped his eyes open. Tension coiled more tightly inside him. He could do without any more bad news today.

Andrea.

Dan exhaled a big breath and reached for calm. He'd let his stepdaughter down by not making time for her before she returned to college last month. They'd talked on the phone on several occasions, but it wasn't the same.

"Hey there, college girl."

"I already hate this semester," Andrea complained.

"The semester has barely begun, honey." Though he and Andrea's mother had divorced, Dan would always think of Andrea as part of his family. Soon he and Jess had to give her the news about the baby.

"Yeah, yeah, I know. It's just that three of my five professors are going to be A-holes."

Dan laughed, the tension that had tightened inside him loosening. "I'm certain they're all top notch professors. Give them time."

"I'll try." Silence echoed for a moment. "That's not really why I called you."

A new kind of worry wove its way through him. "Whatever it is, you know I'll do what I can to help." He had promised Andrea he'd always be there for her—unlike her biological father.

"Good because I really, really need you to do something super important for me."

"Name it."

"Stop working so hard."

He frowned. "Who said I was working too hard?"

"I tried to call you on Friday and then again this morning."

His frown deepened. "I didn't notice any missed calls."

"I didn't call your cell. I called your office in case you were in the middle of something. Shelia said you're working way too hard. She's worried about you. So, you have to stop. You're at that age."

Dan couldn't help himself, he laughed. "I'm not that old, Andrea."

"I'm talking," she said with a harrumph of frustration, "about that age when heart attacks and stuff happen suddenly without any warning. Men your age are under extra stress about their careers and family."

He doubted Shelia had volunteered any information about his current career woes. More than likely, Andrea had come to her own conclusions. Her concern warmed him. "You have my word. I will do my best not to work too hard. Starting today." By the end of the week, he might not have a job.

"How's Jess?"

A smile stretched across his lips. "She's great." Telling Andrea about the baby and wedding plans would have to wait until Jess could be a part of the call. "We've been house hunting."

"You better not be planning a wedding without me," she fussed.

"You'll be the first person we call when the time comes to plan a wedding."

She exhaled a big breath, sounding satisfied. "I love you, Dan. Please take better care of yourself.

One of these days I'll marry some hot guy and I want you to walk me down the aisle."

Now that made him grin. Made him a little weak-kneed, too. Brandon Denton would not be happy about that arrangement. "As long as I get to approve the groom, I'm there."

Andrea told him about her new potential boy-friend, and then she had to go to prepare for an evening class with one of the A-hole professors.

Dan slid the phone back into his pocket. He hoped he could back up the promises he'd made. He'd made some big promises to Jess and to Andrea, and now another person was depending on him. A smile spread across his face when he thought of the baby. He had started to wonder if this day would ever come. Now here they were, he and Jess, preparing for marriage and parenthood all at once.

If Dan could be half the father his had been, he would be contented.

Whether she knew it or not, Jess was going to be an amazing mother. His chest squeezed thinking of her. He loved everything about her. He had since the day he laid eyes on her back in high school. Those rich brown eyes and that gorgeous smile had mesmerized him. He loved the way her blond hair curled if she didn't dry it. She complained about wrinkles and being out of shape, but in truth, she was even more beautiful now than she had been at seventeen. If they had a little girl, he hoped she was the image of Jess.

A light rap at his door drew Dan's attention back to the reality he'd as soon forget. His hard-earned career was in serious jeopardy. "Come in."

The door opened and Lieutenant Clint Hayes walked in. "You wanted to see me?"

Apparently, Dan had wasted his time pulling strings to have Hayes assigned to Jess's team. The man had failed miserably at keeping her close. Then again, Dan didn't know what he'd expected. Jess rarely took orders from anyone.

"You're still having trouble keeping your end of our deal, Lieutenant. I need you to be more proactive."

Hayes studied Dan a moment. "I guess you'll have to talk to my boss then because she has her own ideas about what I need to do."

That was certainly an about face from his attitude only a few days ago, and not the answer Dan wanted to hear. "Are you saying you can't find a way to stay close to her?"

Dan needed to ensure Jess's safety. Wells and Harper were damned fine detectives but they were also Jess's friends. He worried about their emotional involvement clouding their judgment. He wanted someone totally focused on Jess's safety.

"I'm saying," Hayes maintained, "I like my job and I want to keep it."

"You won't lose your job. I'll see to that."

"Can you make that guarantee, Chief? The way I hear it, you may be losing yours."

Fury swept through Dan before he could block it. He tolerated the man's insolence because they both knew what he was demanding fell into a gray area. Dan's method for prompting compliance was coercion, plain and simple. The smart thing would be to dial it back a notch, but this wasn't about being smart, it was about keeping Jess safe.

"Can you do the job or do I need to find someone else? Transfers happen every day, Lieutenant. I can see that you're moved back to Admin as easily as I facilitated your move out."

Anger glittered in the other man's eyes, but to his credit, he held it in check. "I will find a way to do the job."

"Then go do it, Lieutenant."

When Hayes was gone, Dan collapsed into his chair. For the first time in his life, he had no idea how to slow this plunge toward disaster.

CHAPTER SIX

Jess stood back and studied the case board she had made on the expanse of blank wall in her apartment. Her colleagues at the Bureau had always considered her odd for having what she referred to as a homework board. Most people wanted to forget work when they went home. Not Jess. She'd never been able to turn it off that easily.

Amanda Brownfield and her body farm took up a good portion of the wall space behind Jess's sofa. Next to those haunting photos was one of Amanda's mother, several more of the property with its dozens of open graves, and then one of Maddie, the four-year-old daughter Amanda had abandoned.

Jess touched the little blond girl's face. Would she have a little girl? Would she be a good mother? Wasn't motherhood instinctive? What if she didn't possess those instincts? For two decades, her instincts had been so honed in on murder, maybe she was no longer capable of that softer nature. She needed a long talk with Lil. With two kids of her own, Lil had

70

the experience that Jess was sorely lacking. Giving herself credit, she had done pretty well with Maddie. That showed potential, didn't it?

Jess's attention settled on the photo of her father she'd added to the wall only moments ago. She refused to grant any merit to Amanda's suggestion that they shared a father or that he was a killer. They couldn't possibly have any genes in common. Unlike Amanda, Jess had never wanted to harm another human being or animal. The only times she'd ever fired her weapon was when she'd had no other choice. DNA would rule out Amanda's ludicrous claim soon enough.

If her father had gotten involved with the Brownfields, Jess was absolutely certain he wasn't a killer any more than she was. This was another of Spears's illusions to distract her.

Distraction was dangerous. Spears's current tactics kept the investigators who were supposed to be looking for him busy tracking down other killers and sorting through evidence that led back to Jess rather than to him.

You couldn't find what you weren't looking for.

Spears counted on that fact. He was a master at diversion.

Jess moved on to the next photos on her wall. The condemned home in Irondale where Jess and Lily had lived with their parents. Spears had left her a welcome home message there. She should have expected more to come about her past. Her career was all she'd had to lose when this thing with Spears started. When he helped to destroy her career at the Bureau, he hadn't expected her to bounce back so quickly. Thanks to Dan, she had. She'd built a new career and life in Birmingham.

Spears had failed, but he wasn't letting go that easily. He'd turned his attention to her new vulnerabilities: Dan and the child she carried. Like any good strategist, he intended to use those vulnerabilities to achieve his end game. He'd also latched onto how precious the few memories she had of her parents were to her. He'd searched until he found something from her past to exploit.

The accident that took the lives of their parents had always haunted Jess and her sister. The four foster homes had been nightmares in their own right. Her gaze rested on the photo of the Comer Bridge where her parents had died. She hugged herself, feeling cold just remembering the dark water.

She studied the photo of Reverend Henshaw Lori had taken from the DMV database, and then the one from the crime scene where he'd basically been crucified. She wrestled with the emotion that wanted to clog her throat. Why would Spears target him aside from Henshaw's vague connection to her? She hadn't seen him in over thirty years. Could Henshaw have known something about her father? Where did the key fit into the puzzle?

According to what Harper had found so far, Henshaw hadn't been home in two months. There was nothing at his house the key would fit and his cell phone was missing.

Where had the reverend been for the past two months? Staying with a friend? On an extended vacation? No one Harper had questioned had the first clue. The wedding chapel coordinators said he'd performed a ceremony for them last month. They'd called his cell and he had shown up.

Jess stepped closer, adjusted her glasses, and studied Henshaw's photo. "Where have you been, Preacher Gordon?" The fact that he'd gone missing about the same time she returned to Birmingham was significant.

Across the room, her cell clanged. Jess tossed aside the tape she'd been using to post photos and shuffled to the kitchen table. She checked the screen of her cell. *Corlew*. "About time." She hit accept. "Where have you been? I've left you three voicemails."

"Hello to you too, kid."

Jess rolled her eyes. Buddy Corlew was the only person on earth who called her kid. Since he was barely one year older than her that hardly made her a kid compared to him. "I've been trying to reach you all day." Patience was not one of her virtues. "You've been avoiding me."

"You've got me now. What's up?"

He intended to ignore her not so subtle accusation, did he? Setting aside her frustration, she launched into the long list of updates for the man who was supposed to be looking into the crash that killed her parents as well as the trouble Dan was having at the BPD.

"Hell," Corlew growled. "What did Spears have to say this time?"

"*This is where it began, Jess, and this is where it will end.*" She wandered back to the board and stared at the copy of the note Lori had printed for her. No matter that she'd read it twenty times, she shivered.

"He's trying to keep your head spinning, Jess. You know his tactics and motives better than anyone."

Her old friend was right, to a degree. Spears was far too confident to be so wrong. Somewhere amid all this bombardment of evidence from her past was something, he believed to be earthshaking. Jess knew him too well to doubt it.

"It's more than that, Buddy. Eric Spears is a sociopath. He believes he's more brilliant than any of us. Every time he makes a move and we don't catch him, he wins. His moves are carefully planned to ensure success. He thinks he knows something I don't about my father." She hated this feeling of uncertainty. "Is he right?"

Corlew laughed, the sound strained. "He's making you paranoid, kid. The picture of your old man, this Amanda chick, I'm not convinced any of it's real."

"I guess we'll know soon enough." Jess rubbed at the tension lining her forehead. "Sylvia's doing the DNA."

"Good idea. Put your mind at ease. When you have the results, you'll see this is just another diversion Spears has hatched up."

Funny, he didn't sound all that convinced. "There was a retired ABI agent, Randall McPherson, who stopped at the scene today. I tried to talk to him, but he wasn't interested in discussing my parents' accident."

A beat of silence. "McPherson. I've heard of him. I had a client up in Scottsboro when I first started out as a PI. I interviewed the guy once."

"What's his story?" Buddy was keeping something from her. Jess heard it in his voice.

"You know the type. He has his own way. To hell with everyone else."

Jess wasn't buying it. "He knows something, Buddy. *You* know something you're not telling me."

"What I know is something's off, Jess. I'll talk to McPherson. I can't guarantee he'll tell me anything—*if* he knows anything—but I'll rattle his cage."

"Your BPD source told you there was a police report on the accident. We couldn't find it. Why is that?"

"I guess he made a mistake. It happens."

They were going to have a meeting soon. She wanted to see his face when he answered her questions. Maybe she was overreacting, but she had the distinct impression Buddy was hiding something from her.

Jess cleared her head and moved on. "What about the key?" Spears never wasted time or effort on insignificant details.

"I showed the photo you sent me to a picker friend of mine. He knows his junk. Travels all over the country buying antiques like those two guys on TV. He says it's a key to a music box, possibly a jewelry box. Did you or Lily have a music box as kids? Maybe your mom?"

A tune whispered through her. Jess reached for the sofa to steady herself. She squeezed her eyes shut and tried to remember more. Nothing but a few notes from a tune that may or may not have been from a music box would come to her. The idea of a music box felt right.

"I think my mother had one. I'm not certain."

"Did Henshaw visit your home often? Would he have had access to your mother's things?"

Jess stared at the photo of the man. "I'm not sure." Her memories of those years were few and vague but always happy. Had she blocked the bad ones? Repressing bad memories as a child was a common defense mechanism. This was another reason she needed to speak with Lily soon. She couldn't keep protecting her sister from all this. Lil would accuse Jess of doing exactly what she hated other people doing to her—protecting her. And her sister would be right.

"Don't worry about McPherson, Jess. I'll handle him. Stay on the preacher and the key."

"What about your source in the department? Anything new there?" Something helpful, hopefully.

"He's avoiding me like the plague. I have a feeling he's being watched and can't risk contact. Black's got Dan's case locked up tight as a drum."

He. "Are you ready to give me a name yet?"

"How about that Crimson Tide? They stomped all over Mississippi State on Saturday."

Jess rolled her eyes. "I didn't catch the game, Corlew. I was neck deep in dead bodies."

"I can't give you anything else on Danny boy, but know that I'm on it. I'll track down McPherson tomorrow and get back to you."

"You better. Don't make me have to hunt you down, Buddy Corlew."

"Don't tease me, Jess. My heart can't take it."

The call ended and Jess tossed her phone aside. The man might be her oldest friend but he drove her crazy most of the time. Since he was the best PI in Birmingham and one of the few people she trusted, she just had to deal with his eccentric ways.

She needed air. Where was Dan? He should be home by now. She dragged off her glasses and left them on the dining table. The *empty dining* table. Jess winced. She'd been so focused on the homework board she'd forgotten about dinner. At some point, she absolutely had to learn to make food a priority and chocolate didn't count. She was pregnant for heaven's sake!

This morning was a textbook example. She'd expected to have breakfast with Wendell Jones before heading to Scottsboro, but murder had knocked the promised meeting off her calendar. At least when she'd called to cancel their scheduled monthly breakfast meeting, Jones had given her an update on DeShawn Simmons, a young man she'd rescued from kidnappers last month. DeShawn was off to college, fulfilling the hopes and dreams of his grandparents. After that, the day had gone downhill and Jess had grabbed fast food on the run. Good thing she always carried a stash of M&Ms as back up.

"Way to achieve a healthy diet, Jess," she grumbled. She pressed her palm to her belly. "I promise to do better." She should ask Sylvia and Gina about cooking classes. Lil would scold her and say there was only one way to learn: trial and error.

Jamming her feet into her flip-flops, she scrolled through her contacts until she found the number for the neighborhood pizza place that delivered. By the time she reached the landing outside her door, two large pizzas with the works were ordered and charged to her credit card. She shoved her cell into the back pocket of her jeans and descended the stairs, waving to the uniforms watching her place. The least she could do was order pizza for them, too.

Across the driveway, her landlord, George Louis, watered flowers. Guilt made her walk over and say hello. She wasn't used to having a neighbor so involved in her daily life. She'd owned the house in Virginia for almost ten years and hadn't known her neighbors' names. There was no way of avoiding interaction with George Louis. Dan called him nosy. Jess felt certain he was simply lonely. Long retired, he filled his days with yard work and keeping his home in tiptop shape.

"Good evening, George. I ordered pizza, would you like to join us for dinner?"

He glanced at the driveway, noting the absence of Dan's car. "Thank you, Jess. I've had dinner already. It's very kind of you to think of me. Is Dan working late again?"

"Unfortunately." Jess shifted the topic. "You're practically the only person in the neighborhood whose flowers haven't surrendered to the heat. They're still beautiful."

"I don't neglect my duties," he said with a hum of agreement. "Once they're planted, I pay proper attention to their needs. Water, fertilizer, and such. A man should never plant or build anything he can't properly maintain."

"Well, they're lovely, George."

"Will Dan be building or buying a new house?"

"Buying, I think. We looked at a house in Mountain Brook last night but I'm sure we'll be considering many others."

George turned his attention back to his flowers. "I suppose, when the time comes, you'll be moving with him."

George was lonely. Of course, he would hate seeing her go. Then again, after all the drama she'd brought to his life, he might be glad.

"You'll be the first to know when we find something."

"I'll miss you, Jess."

The words were so desolate she couldn't help but feel bad for him. She mustered a smile. "I'll only be in another neighborhood, not another city."

He tinkered with the water hose nozzle. "You'll probably forget all about me."

"Impossible." Jess laughed. "You're a good friend."

Dan arrived and her pulse quickened. "Come on over if you change your mind about the pizza," Jess offered as she backed toward the driveway.

George nodded without looking up.

Jess stalled a few yards from the rental to watch as Dan got out. Her heart skipped a little beat. It was silly, but she had no control over the reaction. He'd always had that effect on her.

As weary as he looked, the smile that appeared just for her squeezed her chest. "Sorry I'm late."

"Pizza's on its way." She fell into step with him, suddenly in a hurry to get inside so she could put her arms around him. "Did Black give you a hard time?"

Dan shrugged. "He did his job."

"It's over now." Jess wished the Allen investigation were resolved. Captain Allen was in all probability dead. Whatever he'd done, he'd crossed the wrong drug lord. You didn't mess with a man like Salvadore or Leonardo Lopez and walk away. They might never find Allen's body or know who killed him.

Inside, door locked and security system rearmed, Jess helped Dan out of his jacket. She pushed her arms around his neck and kissed him. Whatever else was wrong in their lives, this was right.

Dan's lips curved into a smile against hers. "I've been looking forward to this all day."

"Me, too." She ushered him to the sofa. "Sit. You need a beer."

"Does that mean you have something to tell me that I don't want to know?"

Jess smiled at him over the fridge door. "Potentially."

She had been debating whether to tell him about Amanda's claims or not. Why burden him with that worry before the allegations were corroborated. At some point between finding that photo of her father and tonight, Jess had realized her reasoning was wrong. How could she demand that he stop being over protective of her if she was doing the same thing to him?

No, it was more than that. As much as she hoped Amanda's claims about her father were false, the very idea that her father may have led a secret life—keeping his wife and children in the dark and placing them in danger—was disgraceful. Jess didn't want to ever hurt Dan like that, no matter the reason. It was time she told him the part in all this she'd kept to herself.

She grabbed a beer and headed back to the sofa.

He took the cold bottle from her hand, set it aside, and pulled her down next to him. "I'd really like another of those welcome home kisses first."

Something about how he said the words stole her ability to speak. Careful of the healing injury on his forehead, she took his face in her hands and pulled his mouth down to hers. She kissed him gently, until her lips started to tremble, and then she kissed him harder. His arms went around her and he lifted her onto his lap. She wanted the kiss to last forever but the burn of tears warned that she'd better take a moment to pull herself together.

She drew back, licked her lips, loving the taste of him. "I hired Buddy to look into my parents' accident."

Dan trailed a finger down her cheek. "You believe there's something more than what the trooper's report said or is this about Spears fascination with you and your past?"

She braced herself. "One of the photos in that lockbox I found in the Brownfield home was of my father. Amanda says he's *her* father. Sylvia's doing the DNA to…see."

Dan appeared to digest her words, and then he nodded slowly. "Do you think there's some truth to Amanda's story? The photo could've been planted. Spears visited your Aunt Wanda a couple weeks ago. She told you she showed him old family photos. He may have taken one or more."

Jess wilted against his chest. "I don't know. Buddy thinks that's the case."

"Glad Corlew and I are on the same page."

Despite his nonchalant words, she felt the tension in Dan. He and Buddy had been rivals since high school. They were the two hottest guys in Birmingham back then, only from different sides of the tracks. The football rivalry was legendary. On some level, their competitiveness continued into adulthood.

"I should have told you before I told him." After her parents died, she had learned to keep her personal life compartmentalized. First, as a kid so she didn't have to talk about her dead parents or her foster parents and then later in the pursuit of her career. It was easier that way. "I guess I'm as guilty of wanting to protect you as you've been of trying to protect me. With the Allen investigation, Prescott's complaint, and Dority's allegations against you, I didn't want to add this on top of all that until I was sure. I haven't told Lil either."

For an instant disappointment flickered in his eyes, then it was gone. "I'm glad you told me. I know this was about protecting me and not about a lack of trust."

"Of course it wasn't about trust!" The last thing she wanted was for him to feel she didn't trust him. "I couldn't bear the idea of you seeing me in that light." She hadn't admitted that part to herself until a moment ago. "I've worked really hard at not being the poor little orphan girl. Adding a father with a sketchy past is difficult to swallow."

"Jess." He took her hand in his, kissed it gently, the pain she felt reflected in his eyes. "I've never looked at you that way. All I've ever seen is this strong, intelligent, and beautiful woman who stole my heart in high school and still has it."

"It's ridiculous, I know." She blinked at the burn in her eyes. Dammit, she hated getting emotional like this. "I haven't thought about my childhood in decades until now. I should have seen this coming.

We all have our Achilles Heel and Spears found mine."

"You and Lil went through so much as kids." Dan caressed her cheek with the pad of his thumb. "If our children are as strong as the two of you, they'll do well in life."

"Thank you." It was time to come clean with the rest. "There's one more thing you should know about my deal with Buddy."

Dan arched a skeptical brow. "I hope that doesn't mean what I think it means."

"It means," she went on, "he's looking into who's trying to frame you. So is Gina."

"Oh hell, Jess." Dan dropped his head back on the sofa. "The last thing I need is Buddy Corlew trying to fix things for me." He frowned at her, clearly not happy. "Have you forgotten that interview he did with Gerard Stevens? Corlew thinks I screwed him when he was fired from the department. He might be your friend, Jess, but he isn't mine."

How did she explain? "Whatever grudges Buddy held in the past, he doesn't feel that way now. He admires you and wants to help. He knows this is wrong, Dan. I think this entire situation opened his eyes about a lot of things."

Dan was obviously not convinced. "Have you considered that maybe he's the reason things keep getting worse?"

"You have every right not to trust him." She hoped she wasn't that far off the mark about Buddy even if the idea had crossed her mind once or twice.

"Maybe it's time to put the past behind you and see Buddy for who he is now. He was arrested because he was trying to help us, Dan."

"His arrest was related to what you asked him to do?"

Jess nodded. "I think that says a lot, don't you?"

"I'm not making any promises where Corlew is concerned," Dan warned, "but in the future I will attempt to give him the benefit of the doubt."

She couldn't ask for more than that. "Your decision is more than fair."

"I hope you're right about him."

"I am." If, by some bizarre twist of fate, she were wrong, she would make Buddy pay in ways he couldn't fathom in his worst nightmares.

"Gina has plenty of sources, it never hurts to have her on our side."

"That was my thinking." Jess inhaled deeply, loving the scent of him. She traced the pattern on his tie and couldn't wait to help him out of the rest of his clothes.

"Gant and I were playing phone tag all day, any news from him?"

Jess filled him in on Amanda's claims about her meeting with Spears. "Gant is still skeptical, but I believe Spears is right here in Birmingham. If Amanda is telling the truth, he may have Rory Stinnett and Monica Atmore with him."

Dan tucked a wisp of hair behind her ear. "All the more reason for you to be extra careful in all you do, Jess."

Two weeks ago, she would have been annoyed by his advice. "You won't get any argument from me."

He squeezed her hand. "Good."

Her cell chimed and she pulled it from her hip pocket. Hopefully, the pizza was here. The text wasn't about the pizza delivery. *Katherine Burnett.*

"Your mom sent us the addresses of several houses she thinks we should see." Jess showed him the text.

"You talked to Mom about houses?"

"She said she keeps an eye on all the best properties. I thought we could use the help." She forwarded the text to Dan's phone.

The broad smile that broke across his face had her heart fluttering. "I would like that very much."

Jess caressed his strong jaw. "Me, too."

"I was thinking about Jessica for a girl's name." He kissed her chin.

His talented lips moved down her throat and she shivered. "So we're picking out names now, are we?"

"Jessica Lee," he murmured.

Jess smiled. Let Spears keep digging around in her past. Whatever unpleasant truth he found, it didn't change who Jess Harris was.

"I like that name," she whispered between kisses.

By the time the pizza had arrived, they had decided on Daniel Thomas for a boy—as if there had been any question.

This, Jess decided, was normal.

CHAPTER SEVEN

Lori had notes scattered all over the table. It had been another burger and fries dinner night. She felt a little bad that they hadn't found time for a decent meal in days, but this case was getting to everyone on the team.

Chet sat on the other side of the table watching her and sipping his beer. He'd been doing that for the past ten minutes and hadn't said a word.

She looked up at him and smiled. "What?"

"You shouldn't wear that shirt." He nodded to the blue button-down one she'd found in the back of his closet. He'd worn it to Chester's birthday party and then hung it back in the closet without washing it. She'd taken it off the hanger to wash it, but then she'd gotten lost in Chet's scent.

"Why?" She lifted her chin and eyed him boldly. "I like wearing it."

"Seeing you in that shirt makes me want to do things," he warned, "you probably don't want to do right now."

They'd had sex last night and this morning. "Are you saying you want to have sex right now?"

"Now. Later." He shrugged. "Anytime, anywhere."

Her body reacted to his words, going hot in an instant. "We should talk about the case first otherwise we won't get to it."

"Works for me." He allowed his gaze to linger on her lips before going on. "The reverend left perishable food in his fridge. His bed was unmade. Dirty clothes still in the hamper. It's as if he walked out of the house one day and never came back. The neighbors hadn't noticed anything amiss since his grass is cut by a lawn service. He doesn't subscribe to the newspaper so no papers piled up at the door. His mail goes to a post office box."

"He took his cell phone." Lori picked up from there. "So he wasn't trying to hide from everyone."

Chet nodded. "Since we didn't find it, I got a warrant for his phone records. That'll take a couple days. For now, the only calls we can confirm are the ones with the wedding chapel coordinator."

"His wife died twenty years ago. He has no children or close family." Lori ached at the idea of spending part of her life without Chet. That was the thing about falling in love, everything that mattered to you changed. She'd fought it every step of the way. She hadn't been ready, maybe she still wasn't, but she was there—madly, deeply in love with this man. "His church was his only family."

"Henshaw hadn't been to church in two months," Chet countered.

"You're interviewing members of the congregation?"

He nodded. "I spoke to the current pastor and a couple of people he said were close to Henshaw. No one has heard from him. All three have tried calling him with no luck. No one noticed anything unusual about his behavior before he stopped showing up for services. Whatever happened, it was sudden and without warning."

"What about his vehicle?" Lori hadn't noticed anything out of the ordinary in the twelve-year-old Corolla except the evidence that the reverend did a lot of eating in his car.

"Nothing from the lab yet on the Corolla. I don't expect them to find anything." He tossed back another swig of his beer. "Spears and his followers are too smart for that kind of careless mistake."

"You didn't find any connection to the key at his home?"

"If Henshaw had whatever the key unlocked, he took it with him to the chapel." Chet turned the sweating bottle around in his fingers. "Which means, Spears has it now."

Lori exhaled a frustrated breath. "Did you hear anything on Chief Burnett?"

Chet set the bottle aside and pushed his hands through his hair. Lori wished she were closer so her fingers could follow that same path. Watching him move did things to her. Things that made her want to forget about work and climb over this table to get to him.

"Rumor is," Chet shot a disgusted look at the ceiling, "for what that's worth, the powers that be want him out and all this bullshit with the Allen case is making it easy. Prescott's keeping her mouth shut. Her attorney must have warned her to stop slandering Burnett until her complaint is investigated."

Lori wanted to slap that redheaded witch. Lieutenant Valerie Prescott was pissed that she hadn't been promoted and given Allen's position after it became clear he wasn't coming back. Before that, Prescott had been angry about Jess being chosen for the division chief position over SPU instead of her. The lieutenant had it in for Burnett. She was a good cop, but there was more to being a division chief than being a good cop. She lacked the leadership skills necessary to rise to that level, not to mention the personality to inspire others.

"I don't think Prescott's complaint will hold up," Lori argued. "Chief Burnett has always been more than fair."

"No question about that," Chet agreed. "The whole situation definitely sucks for Burnett. He lost his home, the woman he loves is being threatened by a psycho serial killer, and his job is hanging by a thread. Oh yeah, and we can't forget that one of his ex-wives is claiming he was dirty when he worked in the mayor's office."

Lori pushed her notes aside. "Sometimes I hate this job." When justice didn't prevail, it made her want to toss the badge and gun and walk away.

"Speaking of things I hate, Cook signed up for the detective's exam."

Lori wasn't sure which part of what Chet said startled her the most. "You hate Chad?" Chad Cook was a great guy and a good cop. Jess had asked her and Chet to help him prepare for the detective's exam. Unfortunately, there hadn't been time.

"No." Chet knocked back the last of his beer. "I hate Hayes."

Lori frowned. "O…kay. You lost me."

"Hayes has been prepping Cook for the exam. That's why he signed up to take the test."

On one hand, Lori understood she should be grateful that Clint had picked up their slack, but she got what Chet was talking about. "He went behind our backs."

"All he had to do was say, hey, you guys are a little busy right now, so why don't I work with Cook so he's ready for the exam?" Chet shook his head. "No. He keeps it a secret to make us look bad to the chief. I've got that dude's number."

Lori wanted to believe differently but Clint had been going out of his way lately to be an ass. "I don't get it. What does he hope to gain by alienating the two of us?"

"Brownie points with the chief, I guess."

And Lori had given the guy a recommendation. She shook her head and held her hands up. "You know what? Let's give him the benefit of the doubt and chalk it up to being a team player. Forget the hidden agenda and be happy for Cook. He deserves a promotion." It made her feel better to let it go.

"I'll try. No guarantees."

Chet was never going to like Hayes because he'd helped Lori with her sister all those years ago. It wasn't the idea that Clint had helped, it was the shady way he'd gone about it. To some extent, it was jealousy. Her man loved her and she liked that. "Did you hear from Sherry today?"

"She called right before five. This time I got to talk to Chester."

Chet's ex had taken his son and disappeared. She claimed she was afraid of the escalating situation with the Spears case and frankly, Lori believed her. Sherry wanted to protect her son. The problem was she had gone about it the wrong way. She should have discussed the move with Chet first. Chester was his son, too. He should know where the boy was.

Chet deserved better. Lori would never take him for granted. Never. She stood and started unbuttoning the shirt. "Is it hot in here or is it just me?"

Chet grinned. "Hard to say. It's pretty damned hot."

With the shirt hanging open in invitation, she moved around the table and took his hand. "Follow me, Sergeant, I have a couple of new tricks I want to show you."

By the time they reached the bedroom, she'd peeled off his clothes and wrapped her legs around his naked waist. He rolled onto the bed with her still in his arms. On his back, he bracketed her hips with his strong hands and pulled her down onto the part of him that was rock hard. Her body screamed for release but he held her still. Wouldn't let her move. Their desperate gasps for breath were the only sounds.

When she started to squirm, he rolled again, tucking her under him, his body still one with hers. He left a trail of kisses along her throat, massaged her breasts with his long fingered hands. Finally, he drew back, an inch or two, waited and waited…then he sank back into her again.

She came.

He kissed her slowly, his thrusts equally slow until they both shuddered with release.

With her body still quivering, he started all over again.

CHAPTER EIGHT

"I've asked you this once already, Chief Harris, but I'm going to ask you again." Chief Black looked directly at her as if he might change her mind by sheer force of will. "Are you certain you don't want your union rep or your attorney present? Detective Hendrix is right outside the door. He has expressed his concern about my continuing this questioning without his presence."

Jess had known both Deputy Chief Harold Black and Lieutenant Kelvin Roark, his cohort in these proceedings, about the same length of time. She'd met them both in the course of her work as deputy chief of SPU. Roark was Black's second in command, which was the extent of her knowledge of him.

Black, however, she understood perfectly. He didn't like her and he didn't like the way she did things. Mostly, he'd said he didn't like the idea that she brought trouble to Dan. She couldn't discount his concerns. The question was, to what degree were

94

Dan's troubles related to her and the business with Spears versus the result of Black's renewed desire to be chief of police.

There wasn't a doubt in her mind that Mayor Pratt and his cronies had dangled that carrot. Dan was no longer playing by Pratt's rules and the mayor wanted someone who would. Harold Black had been waiting in the wings for years. How far would a man his age, nearing sixty, go to advance the final years of his career and take his retirement pension to the next level?

As for Hendrix, the union rep, she didn't know him at all, but she imagined he and Black were friends. The two probably had a beer together now and again. No, she preferred to keep this investigation into Allen's disappearance among as few people as possible. The more folks involved, the greater the likelihood of leaks.

"Am I a suspect?" Jess tossed out the question to annoy Black. She was a person of interest, of course. There was nothing to challenge there. If he hadn't deemed her a person of interest, Black wasn't doing his job.

Visibly exasperated, the older man sighed. "You are not. We have no suspects in this case at this time. What we do have are several persons of interest, such as yourself. Are we clear on that, Chief Harris?"

"We are absolutely clear, Chief Black."

"On the morning of Friday, August sixth," Black began, "Captain Allen's cell was picked up by a tower near your home address. Did you see Captain Allen at any time that morning?"

"I did not," she said in answer to his question. "I had no idea he'd been anywhere near my apartment until days later."

"Someone tampered with your personal vehicle that morning, and you and Chief Burnett believe it was Captain Allen, is that correct?"

"I believe it was him, yes." She smiled at his blatant attempt to trap her into saying what he wanted to hear. "I can't speak for anyone else."

"You and Captain Allen had disagreements on several occasions, Chief Harris. At any time, did he make any threats to you? Did you report any threats to Chief Burnett?"

"On July 29, I entered a house Captain Allen's Task Force had under surveillance to question Salvadore Lopez. Captain Allen was unhappy with my decision to do so. He informed Burnett about the incident, not me."

"There were other incidents."

Oh, yes. Several. "On August fifth, we were investigating a scene where two low level drug dealers were murdered with a similar MO to the Grayson murder, which I was investigating at the time. Captain Allen didn't care for my line of questioning relative to Detectives Grayson and Riley. Allen made that quite clear." She opted to leave out the part he'd insinuated about her relationship with Burnett being the reason she had her position as well as his warning that she didn't have any friends in the department.

"Did you report this incident to Chief Burnett?"

"I did not. I'm a big girl, Chief Black. I don't go running to the boss every time someone disagrees with me or with my methods. Allen is entitled to his opinions and conclusions."

"So you were well aware of his dislike for how you handle your investigations, is that correct?"

Jess shrugged. "He planted a bomb in the department car I was supposed to use. I was very well aware, yes."

"You had no contact with Captain Allen at any time other than the incidents we have discussed?"

"I did not. Typically, Sergeant Harper contacted him if we were on a case that involved the Gang Task Force. Allen and I didn't interact often."

Black closed the folder in front of him. "Thank you, Chief Harris. If we need anything else, we will contact you. As you know, we're still searching for leads on the case."

Jess picked up her bag and left the room without saying more. There was nothing to say. Captain Ted Allen had been dirty. Whether the investigation ever proved it or not, there was no other explanation for him tampering with her car or for planting a bomb in the department vehicle assigned to her. The only question was why had he decided Jess was his enemy? Yes, she had encroached into his territory, but she hadn't disrupted his surveillance or anything else. Well, not unless you counted telling Leonardo Lopez, the top West Coast drug lord, what his errant children were up to down here in Birmingham.

The one conclusion that made sense was the idea that Allen had been in bed with Salvadore Lopez, Leonardo's son who'd been handling the drug shipments in Birmingham for years. On that score, Jess had waltzed in and crashed the party for Salvadore. Her actions should have been considered a good thing. Apparently, Allen had seen it differently.

"Chief Harris!"

Jess had almost reached the bank of elevators when Detective Hendrix caught up with her. Ignoring him, she pressed the button and watched the numbers light up over the doors.

"All I need is a moment of your time, Chief."

"I'm in a hurry, Detective. What can I do for you?"

"You really shouldn't go into a meeting like that without union representation," he chastised. "That's what I'm here for, Chief. I can protect your rights."

"I appreciate your concern, Detective Hendrix, but I'm not worried. I told the truth. There's nothing in Chief Black's investigation to protect me from."

Hendrix glanced around before leaning closer. "I wish you'd talk to Chief Burnett." He shook his head. "Whether he wants to admit it or not, he's in real trouble. He needs the union behind him."

Jess smiled though she doubted it appeared anymore sincere than it felt. "I'm afraid you'll need to speak with Chief Burnett about those concerns." The chime sounded signaling the elevator had arrived. "Good day, Detective."

She supposed she should have allowed Hendrix to escort her back to the office since she wasn't supposed to go anywhere—not even from office to office—alone. *Just this once wouldn't hurt.*

Before she could board the elevator, her cell rang. She didn't recognize the number. "Harris."

"Chief, we finally located the owner of the Impala."

Sheriff Foster. At this rate, she was going to have to add him to her contact list. "Have you questioned him?" She changed her mind about the elevator, not wanting to risk the call dropping, and headed for the stairwell.

"He's dead. So is his girlfriend. We're at the scene now. I thought you might want to head this way. It looks like there might be a connection to you beyond that note after all."

"I'll be there as quickly as possible, Sheriff. Thank you for calling."

Two hours. There was no way to get to Scottsboro more quickly without a helicopter. The department had one but Black would accuse her of wasting department resources.

Jess hurried down to the SPU office. Cook and Hayes should already be in Scottsboro by now at the Brownfield farm. Harper was tracking down what Henshaw had been up to the past couple of months and Lori was checking into McPherson's background. There was something more going on with McPherson. Whatever Buddy knew or thought he knew he obviously wasn't ready to share it yet.

SPU resources were spread thin. While Black and Roark were overseeing the coordination of resources and information related to the Spears investigation with the Bureau, Jess and her team were scrambling to put together the pieces that connected Spears to the homicides related to her past. Sadly, all those resources were coming up with zero. Based on previous experience, they could have an army of investigators and Spears wouldn't be caught unless he wanted to be. He would continue his game until he had accomplished what he wanted, and then he would disappear.

Not this time, Spears.

Jess ran into Hayes outside her office door.

"You're back." He acted surprised to see her.

"I thought you and Cook would be in Jackson County by now." Had something else happened that she hadn't heard about?

"Detective Wells wanted to go with Cook." Hayes lifted one shoulder in a blasé shrug. "She said something about needing to have a second look inside the farmhouse. Is that a problem?"

"No." Jess frowned, hating that the reaction would only add more lines to her face. "I'm just surprised she didn't check in with me first." Jess appreciated having a team she could trust to follow through and make the necessary decisions. Lori had earned her trust and respect. Harper and Cook had as well. Hayes was a work in progress. He had pulled a stunt or two that had her wondering if he wanted to make it through his six-month probationary period in SPU. He was a good detective and a very intelligent man. She had high hopes he would curb that slightly arrogant attitude and toe the line. Until then, she wouldn't be giving him the same leeway she gave the others who had earned that privilege.

"Cook needed to get on the road and we weren't sure how long you'd be," Hayes offered by way of explanation for the change in plans.

"No problem. I'll check with Lori later." Her stomach warned she should have had more than yogurt this morning. A handful of the M&Ms she carried in her bag would have to do. "We're headed that way as well, Lieutenant. Sheriff Foster found the owner of the Impala."

"Has the owner given up anything yet?" Hayes grabbed his suit jacket and started toward the door where Jess waited.

"The owner's dead. We'll have to find our answers without his help."

Hayes hesitated at the door, probably because she kept standing there staring at the case board and all those photos of dead people—murder victims. Then there was her father and Amanda...and Maddie.

"Was there something else before we go?"

Jess blinked, then shook her head. "I'm ready, Lieutenant."

Before this day was done, she intended to visit Maddie. Jess knew exactly how it felt to suddenly be taken from all you knew. That little girl needed to see a familiar face.

In the parking garage, she settled into the passenger seat of Hayes' Audi and fastened her seatbelt. Her hands lingered at her waist. She'd had a heck of a time fastening her skirt this morning. Before long, she was going to have to retire her few and favorite suits, like this brown one, until post pregnancy.

Shopping couldn't be ignored forever.

As soon as she got caught up, she had to make that happen.

By then she might be naked.

SOUTH HOUSTON STREET, SCOTTSBORO
12:35 P.M.

Eli Mooney, Caucasian, sixty-seven, and his girl-friend, Marla Skelton, Caucasian, sixty-two, had been dead at least twenty-four hours. Their home was a small cottage style house with generous porches on the front and back. The yard was a little overgrown and, at the moment, cluttered with official vehicles.

Inside there was lots of wood paneling and vinyl flooring throughout. Gun racks and mounted deer heads hung on the walls of the living room. A survey of the kitchen revealed a generous supply of beer in the fridge and a freezer packed with venison. A good hunter was proud of his kill and never wasted the animal. According to one of the deputies, Mooney was an experienced hunter as well as a skilled taxidermist.

The tables had turned at some point yesterday, and Mooney and his girlfriend had become the prey.

Fully clothed in jeans and a tank top, his girlfriend, Skelton, had a single gunshot wound to the back of the head, execution style, up close with a small caliber weapon. Probably a .22. She lay face down on the kitchen floor.

The smell of blood and feces was intense. Dressed in cut-off shorts and a T-shirt, Mooney was seated at the table. His right arm was braced on the tabletop with a beer in his hand. Blood had sprayed across the table and pooled on the floor around his chair.

The killer had painstakingly sutured Mooney's lips, and then with a single deep stroke of a blade, opened his throat from one carotid artery to the other.

Foster had kept the evidence techs out until Jess arrived. Hayes was videoing the scene with his cell phone while Jess studied the killer's work.

"Looks like the murder weapon in the sink."

Jess had a look at the bloody hunting knife lying against the stained white porcelain. "I'll bet he didn't leave us any prints."

Hayes chuckled. "I'd say that's a given."

Jess returned to the table and checked the victim's hand clutching the can of beer. "His fingers were glued to ensure they stayed in place." The same method used on the reverend's hands.

Since retiring as the high school janitor, Mooney supplemented his income as a taxidermist with most of his business from local hunters. Lately, people had started bringing their deceased pets to him as well, opening up a new market and source of revenue.

Jess needed to see if there was anything in his mouth. For that, she needed the coroner. "Sheriff, can you call the coroner? I'd like him to remove these sutures so we can see if there's anything inside Mr. Mooney's mouth."

"Adams just rolled up, Chief. I'll have one of my deputies get him on in here for you."

"Thank you, Sheriff."

While Foster gave the order via his radio, Jess studied the victim. Like Henshaw, Mooney's mouth had been sewn shut while he was still alive. The blood trail down his chin and throat left no question. The can of beer, a Bud Light likely from the twelve pack in the fridge, was unopened.

"Where did Mr. Mooney do his taxidermy work?" Jess asked when Foster had tucked his radio away. If he had a shop at a different location, Jess wanted to have a look there as well.

"There's a workshop out back. My deputies are checking it out now." Foster shook his head. "Other than a few barroom brawls and the occasional traffic violation, Mooney was never in any kind of trouble. I can't figure out how he got mixed up in whatever the hell this is."

Jess wished she knew the answer to that one as well.

Foster's radio crackled. He pulled it free of his utility belt. "Did you find something, Woods?"

"You better come on out here and see this for yourself, Sheriff," came the deputy's response. "Bring those Birmingham cops, too. This is crazy, Sheriff."

"On our way." Foster winced. "Sounds like he's a little excited."

"I'm certain they don't see crime scenes like this every day." Jess remembered her first big crime scene. Three men had robbed a bank, and then couldn't agree on how to split the proceeds. They'd ended up killing each other.

On the far side of the kitchen was a door that led to the back porch. Jess paused long enough to remove her shoe covers but kept the gloves on. She hurried across the porch and backyard to keep up with Hayes and Foster's long strides. The workshop sat about thirty yards behind the house. At the door, she and Hayes donned more shoe covers though no one else bothered. It was too late to do anything about that now.

The building appeared to be one large room. Shelves filled with the various tanning chemicals and preservatives Mooney used in his work lined one wall. Examples of his taxidermy work: a bobcat, a couple of squirrels, a rattlesnake, and a deer head were mounted on the opposite wall. A long metal worktable occupied the center of the room. On the far end of the workshop were large metal sinks, the kind used in restaurants. Next to the sink was another door. The two deputies who'd been exploring the building waited there.

"You're not gonna believe this." A deputy—Woods, Jess recognized his voice—motioned to the door. A pair of bolt cutters lay on the floor alongside a lock that had been cut free. "We didn't go inside," Woods, said. "We just looked and...well, see for yourself."

Hayes led the way through the door with Jess close behind him. There was another table in the center of this room, but this one looked more like the ones found in an embalming room. On closer inspection, Jess decided it was an embalming table. More shelves lined the wall beyond the table. Glass jars of varying sizes stood on the shelves. As her brain registered what floated in those many, many jars, Jess reminded herself to breathe. Organs... body parts. *Human.* She moved toward the shelves, needing a better look to make sure what she saw was the real thing.

Human hands, feet, hearts, ears, eyeballs...definitely real.

"Chief."

Slowly, hardly able to take her eyes from the rows and rows of human parts, she turned to face Hayes. He was staring at the wall that separated this room from the rest of the building. She'd been so focused on the embalming table and then the jars, she hadn't looked back to see what was on that wall as she entered the room.

For one second, she stood there staring. Mounted on the wall in different poses were bodies—*human* bodies. There were three young women, one middle-aged man, and one elderly woman. All were nude and perfectly preserved.

"Holy hell," Foster muttered as he and his deputies came through the door to see what had captured Jess's attention.

"That right there," Deputy Woods said, pointing at the older woman, "is his momma. She died last year."

"Do you recognize the others?" Jess asked, her voice sounding a little hollow. It had been a while since she'd run into a Norman Bates wannabe.

"Not right off," Foster admitted. He turned to his deputy. "We're going to need some of those forensic fellas from Huntsville, too."

"Sheriff!"

The guy who rushed into the room was a forensic tech, Jess decided. His T-shirt was emblazoned with *CSI Guys Do it Best.*

"Did Adams find something?"

The tech held up an evidence bag. "He pulled this note from Mooney's mouth."

Jess moved toward Foster as he took the bag. He shook his head and passed it to her. She read the words handwritten by Spears. *Quite a nasty fellow, this one. He's been keeping a little something for you, Jess.*

Jess passed the note to Hayes for documentation before walking back to the other side of the room to inventory the jars. If Mooney was keeping something for her, she had a bad feeling it was in one of these jars.

Something similar to a label appeared to be attached to the back of each jar. She reached for one, lifted it from the shelf, and turned it around. The label was actually a Polaroid photo. Her pulse started racing as she checked more of the jars. Some of the people in the photos wore clothes from decades gone by. One or two Jess was sure she recognized from the photos found in the lockbox at the Brownfield farm. Had Mooney been a friend of Amanda's grandfather?

Hayes joined her.

"Lieutenant, call Agent Gant and let him know what we've found here."

"Making the call now."

"I don't understand this." The sheriff's face looked as somber as his voice sounded. "How could all this have been going on for so long in my county without me hearing something?"

"We rarely recognize the face of evil," Jess assured him, "unless we catch it in the act or find some evidence that leads us to it."

While Hayes updated Gant, Jess continued to inventory the jars, snapping photos of the contents as well as the Polaroids with her cell phone. When she reached the next row, she hesitated. "Sheriff, do you know if Mooney was related to the Brownfield family?" If not, maybe the family business extended to friends. There had to be a connection.

"Hell if I know," Foster confessed. "It's a small town. Everyone knows everyone else. At least that's what I've always thought. I guess I didn't know some as well as I thought."

"Chief." Hayes had concluded his call and had stalled at the other end of the row of shelves Jess was currently working her way down.

Though he and Jess hadn't worked together for that long, she instinctively recognized the combination of dread and disbelief on his face.

She closed the distance between them, her nerves fraying a little more with each step. A sticky note was fixed to the wide-mouth quart jar that had caught his attention. The note, again handwritten by Spears, was for her.

This is the one you're looking for, Jess.

In the jar was a human fetus, approximately ten inches long, ten or twelve ounces, probably twenty or so weeks based on the development chart she'd seen at the doctor's office last week. Jess's mouth felt dry. Her body felt cold. She moistened her lips and said, "Turn it around."

Hayes did as she asked. Like all the other jars, there was a photo attached to the back, but this photo was different from the others.

This was a photo of her mother.

Jess couldn't get out of the building fast enough. Hayes stayed right behind her. No doubt ready to catch her if she fell apart.

She refused to fall apart.

Her head was spinning. Her stomach was churning. And her chest was hurting, but she would not fall apart.

Her mother wasn't pregnant when she died. Was she? Wouldn't she have told Jess and Lil? Wouldn't there have been a celebration?

Outside, she stumbled to the middle of the yard, and then set her hands on her hips trying to steady herself. She drew in a lungful of fresh air. When she could speak, she turned to Hayes. "Lieutenant, ask Sheriff Foster to round up the coroner or mortician—whoever was responsible for preparing my parents' bodies for transport to Birmingham thirty-two years ago." Fury and pain roared through her. "I want to know the names of everyone who touched their bodies until they arrived at the funeral home in Birmingham."

"I'll take care of it. Would you like to sit down, Chief?"

"I'm perfectly fine, Lieutenant. Are you suggesting otherwise?"

He moved his head from side to side. "No, ma'am."

"Good, because I'm fine. Perfectly fine."

Her lips started to tremble first and then it was her legs. Suddenly, she couldn't hold her weight anymore.

Hayes caught her before she hit the ground.

He was saying something but Jess couldn't make out the words. All she could hear was that damned music box tune…the one she'd only just remembered her mother kept on her dresser.

Then the world went black.

CHAPTER NINE

From the driveway across the street, Buddy Corlew watched the home belonging to retired ABI Agent Randall McPherson. McPherson had made a trip to the Liberty Restaurant for breakfast. He hadn't spoken to anyone except the waitress. He'd read the newspaper and then returned home.

While McPherson had satisfied his appetite under the observant eye of Buddy's colleague, he had gotten into position at a neighbor's home. The neighbor, a woman, lived alone and worked at a drugstore downtown. She wouldn't be home for several hours. The dense shrubs and trees lining her driveway provided good cover for Buddy's Charger and gave him an optimal spot for surveillance. After getting into position, he'd had a look around outside McPherson's house while the guy was still at breakfast.

Now all Buddy had to do was bide his time until the man left the house again.

According to the conversation McPherson had with a caller about ten minutes ago, he would be heading out for lunch shortly. Even better, he was taking his dog with him. Buddy liked dogs. He had one of his own and went out of his way not to harm anyone's pets. Chicks liked guys with dogs, but it made his job a lot less complicated if there weren't any dogs standing between him and his goal.

He adjusted the parabolic listening device. The thing looked and operated a lot like a handheld satellite dish that amplified sound and fed it into the headphones he wore. God bless the inventor who came up with this handy device.

The toilet flushed inside McPherson's house, and then he summoned his dog. The two exited the front door, climbed into the truck parked in the driveway, and drove away. Buddy stowed his tools and waited.

Ten seconds, then twenty, finally a full minute later, the signal Buddy had been waiting for sounded in the earpiece of his wireless communications link.

"Subject has turned west on Willow Street."

"Going in." Buddy climbed out of the Charger, closed the door quietly, and set the security system. If anyone approached his vehicle, he would know it. He paused at the street. Coast was clear so he hustled across and walked around to the back of the house. The back door would be a breeze to open. He'd found no sign of a home security system.

As breaking and entering went, an amateur could have handled this one.

The phone in his hip pocket vibrated. He checked the screen. *Jess*. He couldn't talk to her right now. It was easier to lie to her when he wasn't in the middle of breaking the law. If he found what they needed to clear up the mystery surrounding her parents' deaths, she would forgive him for a couple of minor omissions and deviations from the law.

If he didn't find what he needed, she would never know.

A few quick flicks with the right tools and the back door was unlocked. Silence waited inside the house. The rear entry led into a small kitchen. The laundry room was to the right, living room directly ahead. Beyond the living room was a small box of a hallway flanked by two bedrooms and one bath. No surprises in any of the rooms.

The decorating scheme consisted mostly of blandly painted walls, out of date carpeted floors, and well-worn furnishings.

Buddy started in McPherson's bedroom. He systematically went through a mental checklist to ensure he didn't miss anything. Walls, ceiling, and floor. The furnishings were next. Piece by piece he checked for any potential hiding places. People liked stowing treasures and private papers under the mattress or inside the box springs. Buddy found no access points in the fabric. The backs of dressers and chests were clear. Drawers, inside and all around were as well. He checked the pockets of hanging clothes and inside shoes. The HVAC vents were another popular hiding place. He checked for loose places in the carpet, behind switch and receptacle plates, and then he inspected the overhead light fixture as well as lamps.

Nothing in McPherson's bedroom, so he moved on to the next. Thirty-two minutes were required to check every room except the kitchen. No old work files, no personal files or anything else of interest anywhere in the house so far.

He saved the kitchen for last since it was also his egress. He'd have a look in the old shed on the far side of the small backyard, but he doubted a guy who'd spent his career investigating cases for the Alabama Bureau of Investigation would leave anything important in a rickety old shack. A wood privacy fence weathered by years of cold winters, hot summers, and a lack of attention enclosed the backyard.

The kitchen was typically the most time consuming room. Thankfully, a linoleum floor eliminated the potential for hiding places. A man had no leeway for camouflaging a hidden access with linoleum. The cabinets were another story. Each item inside, boxed and canned, had to be inspected. Either one could be a hiding place made to look as if it had come right off the shelf of the local Kroger.

Seventeen minutes and a healthy sweat later, Buddy still came up empty handed.

He surveyed the room. "I always did love a challenge."

He exited McPherson's home, locking the back door behind him. His cell vibrated again. *Jess.* "Sorry, kid. I'll make it up to you later."

Forty-nine minutes and counting had elapsed since McPherson had driven away. This guy could decide to come home anytime now. Rosey would let Buddy know. He could use a half dozen guys like Rosey, but they didn't come along every day. It took a certain level of trust in the PI business. Most of the ones willing to cross lines and bend rules couldn't be trusted.

Roosevelt, aka Rosey, Cunningham would do anything Buddy asked and never tell another living soul about it. If the man ever failed to show up for the job, Buddy knew to check the morgue. He was that dependable.

A long, slow sweep of the backyard had Buddy wondering if there was an underground bunker around here. Rosey hadn't found any other property in the area owned or rented by McPherson. If he possessed anything to hide, it had to be here unless he used a safety deposit box at the bank. That was always a possibility and a whole other can of worms.

His attention settled on the dilapidated shed. Might as well have a look. "Never judge a book by its cover, Corlew."

The shed leaned to one side as if it might collapse now rather than later. No windows and only one door with a padlock. Buddy removed his lock pick set from his back pocket and went to work. A few seconds later, he removed the padlock. Checking carefully for trip wires first, he pushed the door inward. Hot, stuffy air floated out from the darkness of the shed's interior to greet him.

He'd already leaned into the space when something near his feet caught his eye. Backing up a step, he crouched down to have a look. A grin split his lips. "Well, well. Now we know where you keep your secrets, Mac."

Two sensors had been imbedded in the doorframe, one at about ankle level, the other fifteen or sixteen inches higher. The holes in the facing on either side were no bigger than a dime. A low voltage invisible beam running across the width of the door opening worked similar to one on an overhead garage door. If the beam was disrupted, a signal of some sort was triggered. In this case, an alarm likely went to McPherson's cell.

Buddy checked the rest of the doorframe very carefully before giving it a go. He stepped high over the top sensor, straddling the invisible beam. Once he was inside, he dragged the flashlight from his belt and clicked it on. Turning on any of the light fixtures in the shed might trigger an additional alarm.

Desk, computer, file cabinets, bookcase, and a couple of large bulletin boards loaded with notes and photos filled the ten by twelve space.

"Nice set up."

Buddy pulled out his mini video camera and documented the massive amount of material on the bulletin boards. When that was accomplished, he moved on to the desk. Computer was password protected. He had no time to deal with that. He combed through the desk drawers, checking all the usual hiding places, and then he moved on to the file cabinets. He found plenty, but not what he was looking for.

Annoyed, he stared at the bookcase. Not much beyond a few books and a couple of awards on the dusty shelves. Spotting something on the floor, he squatted down to have a closer look. The thin layer of dust that covered the rest of the floor was swept away from the front of the bookcase.

"Well, well, what have we here?" Buddy stood, got a firm grip on the bookcase, and eased it away from the wall. Beneath it was a small door in the floor, similar to a built-in floor safe only this one was homemade and had a lock instead of a combination.

"Sweet."

The lock took a little longer than the one on the door, but he managed. He opened the safe that was about twelve by twenty-four inches and had a look inside. The concrete hole held file folders. He pulled them out a few at a time. There were only about twenty, and all were clearly labeled and filed in alphabetical order.

"I do love OCD people."

Anyone who pilfered through the files at Buddy's office would be in for an unnerving endeavor. He preferred the relevance method of filing. Depending on how relevant it was to him, the closer to the front of the drawer the case was filed.

In his opinion, it worked fine and dandy most days.

He heaved a frustrated breath. No Brownfield in the B's. No Harris in the H's. He flipped through each folder to ensure the labels weren't intended to mislead anyone doing exactly what he was doing. No such luck.

There had to be something here. Once he had everything back in place, he returned to the bulletin boards. A piece at a time, he removed the material posted there and checked the backsides of the photos and documents. Halfway across the bigger of the two boards, he hit pay dirt.

He moved the calendar pinned to the board and found photos hidden beneath it. One of Margaret Brownfield, another of Amanda as a kid about the age of Maddie, and the coup de grace—Lee Harris. The next photo gave Buddy pause. This one was of Jess and Lil at the funeral with their Aunt Wanda.

"What the hell were you up to, McPherson?"

"What's the answer worth to you?"

Buddy spun around to face the voice. *McPherson.* The big guy filled the open doorway, a nine millimeter leveled on his target—*Buddy.*

"There's a tiny motion sensor behind my desk." McPherson made a sound that wasn't really a laugh. "I guess you missed it."

"Guess I did." Buddy itched to go for his own weapon, but he decided against it considering the old guy was probably a crack shot.

"Your friend's going to be disappointed in himself when he figures out the decision to watch my truck was the wrong decision."

Buddy shrugged. "We all make mistakes."

"Some make bigger ones than others." McPherson pressed the muzzle against Buddy's forehead. "You made a very large error, pal. You should never underestimate your opponent."

CHAPTER TEN

Jess sipped the icy cold Coca-Cola slowly. The weakness and dizziness were subsiding. On some level, she wanted to deny her reaction had anything to do with what they'd found at the Mooney crime scene, but that would be a lie. There was no denying her emotions had gotten the better of her.

She toyed with a French fry. A quick stop at the drive-thru window of the local Jack's and she'd forced down a burger. Not that she'd felt like eating, Hayes had insisted. No, that wasn't right. He'd blackmailed her into eating. She would eat or he would call Dan and tell him what happened. Since Dan had enough to worry about right now, she had chosen the former.

"Feeling better?" Hayes inquired, knowing the answer before he asked.

"Yes." Jess stuffed the fries in the bag and reached for the Coke again. "I guess you were right and all I needed was lunch."

"I did something right for once. I should mark this day on my calendar."

120

"Ha ha." She stretched her neck, wished she could ease the tension there. What the hell was taking Foster so long? He should have called by now.

Jess gazed out over the water. Ironically, it seemed to calm her. She hadn't had a clue where they were going when Hayes swung through for the burgers, and then took off for what he called a quiet place. He was right. The park was basically deserted. He'd parked under a group of trees and rolled the windows down. The breeze coming off the water felt good against her face.

"I have no idea if the coroner I need to question is still alive." She didn't remember his name. Years ago she'd read his report, which had actually been nothing more than a death certificate. Coroners in Jackson County weren't forensic or medical professionals, they were elected officials. At the time of her parents' accident, the coroner was most often the funeral director. Blood Alcohol Tests, if deemed necessary, were run locally to determine if a deceased driver had been under the influence. If an autopsy was needed, the body was sent to a state forensics laboratory.

"I'm guessing we'd know something by now if he were dead."

"You're probably right." She frowned. "I'm surprised we haven't had an update from Wells or Cook." Jess reached to fasten her seatbelt. "Maybe we should drop by the Brownfield farm while we're waiting."

"You were going to check back with Foster to ensure he released that one piece of evidence to BPD. I can call him if you'd like."

"I'll call him. It'll give me an excuse to see where he is on finding the coroner for me." She reached for her cell. "Meanwhile, let's drive over to the Brownfield farm."

While Hayes pointed his Audi in the proper direction, Jess put through a call to Foster. The sheriff explained that he'd been about to call her.

"I have that coroner for you, Chief Harris, and we've prepared the evidence you requested for transport."

Surprised, Jess glanced at Hayes. "Great. We'll be right there."

Hayes executed a U-turn. The BPD cruiser that was her surveillance detail for the day did the same.

Jess took a deep breath and steadied her nerves. As hard as this part was, she had to figure out how Mooney and the…fetus played into Spears's game besides the shock value and the purpose of distracting her.

There had to be something he wanted her to see. There always was.

SCOTTSBORO POLICE DEPARTMENT,
3:10 P.M.

"Harvey Larimore retired as corner twenty years ago, but he didn't retire from the family owned funeral business until about five years ago," Foster explained. He hitched his head toward the elderly man who waited in the interview room. "He's eighty-three years old. No criminal record. Deacon in the church he's attended for better than seventy years."

"He was a mortician?" Jess kept her focus on the questions she needed to ask and not the reason why.

"For most of his life. He started working with his father as soon as he was tall enough to see over the embalming table."

"Family?"

Foster shook his head. "Outlived his wife and both his kids. He lives alone over on Scott Street in the same house where he grew up."

Jess glanced at the sheriff. "Don't tell me," she guessed. "The family home was the funeral home."

"Yes, ma'am. Larimores have been putting folks to rest around here for a hundred years. In that same house until just a few years ago."

A new kind of determination kicked in. "The evidence I'm taking custody of, do you have that handy?"

"I'll have it waiting for you when you finish your interview with Larimore."

"I'd like to take it in with me, please."

For a second or two she thought Foster would question her reasoning, instead he shrugged. "I'll round it up."

"Did you tell him?" Jess asked, stopping the sheriff before he was out the door of the observation room.

Foster glanced at the man waiting beyond the glass. "I told him we had some questions for him about his work at the funeral home. I didn't mention anything else."

"Thank you, Sheriff."

Jess watched Larimore for a while longer, assessing his body language. A tall man, his shoulders were broad and straight despite his age. His overall physical condition looked quite good. He had a full head of gray hair and was well dressed in khakis and a white polo. His hands were wide and remarkably steady. The idea that he had touched her parents' bodies tried to invade her appraisal, but she forced it back. The elderly man showed no outward indication of anxiety as he waited.

Foster reentered the tiny room. "Here you go, Chief. Your detective signed the necessary paperwork already."

Jess accepted the small Styrofoam tote, the kind labs used to transport specimens. "Thank you. Let's not keep Mr. Larimore waiting any longer."

Foster opened the door to the interview room and waited for Jess to go in first. Like all the others she'd ever been inside, the walls were a shade of white, and the serviceable commercial grade tile floor was beige. The table and chairs were more plastic than metal and had seen better days. Nothing about the room was designed to excite the person being interviewed, and there was nothing to focus on other than the law enforcement officer conducting the interview.

She walked directly to the small table in the center of the room and took a seat across from Mr. Larimore. She placed her bag on the floor on one side of her, the tote on the other. "Good afternoon, Mr. Larimore. I'm Deputy Chief Jess Harris from

Birmingham PD. I appreciate you taking the time to speak with me this evening."

He eyed her speculatively. His eyes were pale, far too light to be considered brown. Gold, she decided. The eyeglasses made his eyes look far larger than they actually were.

"You look familiar to me. Have we met before?"

Sheriff Foster pulled a chair up at the end of the table. "She used to be with the FBI, Harv. She's been all over the news for weeks now."

Harv. So the sheriff and Larimore were well acquainted. As Foster had said before, Scottsboro was a small town where everyone knew everyone else. Before Jess could ask her first question, Larimore shook his head.

"Don't think it was the news." He narrowed his gaze as if trying harder to recall where he'd seen her.

"Mr. Larimore, did Sheriff Foster make you aware of your rights?"

One gray eyebrow hiked up higher than the other. "Does he need to?"

Jess smiled, hoping to appear at ease despite the whirlwind of emotions making her jittery. She crossed her feet at the ankles to prevent them from tapping. "I find it's best to take care of that right up front. They teach us to be extra cautious in the FBI." Might as well blame it on the Bureau.

Larimore turned to Foster. "What about it, Sheriff?"

Foster cleared his throat and recited the Miranda rights. When he'd finished, Larimore waved him off. "I don't need no blood-sucking lawyer. Now," he fixed that pale gaze back on Jess, "what do you want to ask me?" He tapped his temple. "Got a mind like a steel trap. Give me a name. If I prepared them for eternal rest, I can tell you everything there is to know about their final journey."

Jess squeezed her hands together in her lap and ignored the way her throat tightened. "Thirty-two years ago there was an accident at Comer Bridge. You took care of the victims."

He nodded. "Most likely. There've been a few accidents around that bridge. I don't always recall the exact date but I never forget a name or a face."

"Lee and Helen Harris."

He stared at Jess for a long moment, and then he smiled. "That's it. She must have been your mother. You look just like her."

Another wave of emotion washed over her. Jess steadied herself. "Did you pronounce them dead at the scene and have their bodies transported to your funeral home to await further instructions from the family?"

"Who else?" Larimore glanced at Foster. "I was the coroner and the funeral director."

"How long were their bodies in your possession?" Jess wished she had a drink of water, but she didn't want anything to break the moment.

"Let's see." Larimore furrowed his brow in concentration. "The accident happened on a Friday afternoon, and the funeral home in Birmingham didn't make it up here until Monday. I cleaned them up, out of respect you know, put their clothes and personal possessions in bags, draped the bodies with fresh clean sheets, and stored them in the cooler."

"Did you discover anything unusual among their personal possessions?"

Larimore shook his head. "A wallet and some change. If your mother had a purse, it must have been left in the car."

Jess's heart bumped her sternum. "Beyond the services you described providing, was any other examination or procedure performed while the bodies were in your custody?"

He shook his head. "No need. State Trooper said it was an accident. Single car. One of those freak things, you know. The driver lost control of the vehicle. I listed the manner of death as accidental. Cause of death was consistent with drowning. White froth in the mouth and nose. Skin was wrinkled from being in the water. No reason whatsoever to send them over to the lab for an autopsy."

She tightened her ankles when one foot jerked. "There were no other injuries to the bodies?"

"Only the expected bruising from the seatbelts."

Jess steadied her hand when it trembled as she reached down for the Styrofoam tote. She placed it on the table, removed the top, then the jar, and sat it on the table. "Can you explain to me, Mr. Larimore, how this, along with numerous other body parts from other victims, made their way into Eli Mooney's workshop?"

Larimore stared at the jar then reared back, anger sparking in his eyes. "Are you telling me that you found such as this in that low down, no account's possession?"

"You have a beef with Mooney?" Foster was visibly startled by Larimore's reaction.

The former coroner swung a now furious gaze toward Foster. "I fired that no good snake in the grass fifteen years ago."

Foster and Jess exchanged a look. "He worked for you?" she managed to ask without her voice quivering.

Larimore scoffed. "He was my janitor. He wasn't supposed to go near the bodies. Never! I warned him that even looking at them was a sin. Wasted my breath. I caught that devil taking pictures. I fired him on the spot. Beat the hell out of him first."

"Why didn't I hear about this?" Foster demanded. "I was already a deputy back then."

"I didn't want that kind of gossip floating around. I told Mooney if I ever heard any talk or saw any photos go public, I'd kill him." He shook his head. "I might be an old man, but that SOB is a dead one! You hear me, Sheriff, I'm going to kill him. I should've killed him when I caught him taking those pictures!"

"Somebody already did, Mr. Larimore," Jess announced. "What I need to know from you is if Eli Mooney had the opportunity and means to do this without leaving behind any evidence of the deed." She gestured to the jar.

"That moron? Impossible?" Larimore visibly wilted. "My son, on the other hand, would've known exactly how to do it. That boy got nearly all the way through medical school before flunking out his final semester." He closed his eyes and shook his head. "God have mercy on his soul. He and Mooney were bosom buddies. They're no doubt both burning in hell right now."

"His son died ten years ago," Foster explained.

Jess couldn't summon any sympathy for his loss. "Was it customary practice at your funeral home to perform an internal examination on a victim?"

Larimore removed his glasses and rubbed his eyes. "Certainly not."

"Did you notice anything at all unusual about my parents' bodies or perhaps something the State Trooper or others involved with the recovery said?"

"Nothing at all." He settled his glasses back into place and rested his gaze on Jess.

"Did…" She moistened her lips. "Did my mother appear pregnant?" The coroner certainly hadn't mentioned the possibility.

"She was small, like you, Chief Harris. If she was pregnant, she wasn't showing at all."

"I appreciate your cooperation, Mr. Larimore." Jess stood. "I may have additional questions for you at another time."

"Whatever you need." He shook his head and muttered more scorching oaths under his breath.

Jess turned to Foster. "Sheriff, may I have a word with you?"

"Sure thing." To Larimore he said, "I'll be right back, Harv. We'll figure out what to do next then."

With her bag draped on one shoulder, Jess placed the jar back into the Styrofoam tote, incredibly without her hand shaking. Foster picked it up before she could and then held the door for her to exit the interview room.

In the corridor, Foster passed the tote to Hayes.

Jess struggled to hang onto her composure. There were several things she needed to do, but the one at the top of her priority list was getting back to Birmingham. First, though, she needed to ensure she and Foster were on the same page. "Sheriff, you and Mr. Larimore, assuming all these body parts came from the Larimore Funeral home, have your work cut out for you. I don't envy you this task."

Foster planted his hands on his hips and shook his head. "I've never seen anything like it, that's for sure."

"This morning Amanda Brownfield mentioned that her grandfather had friends." Jess glanced at the tote the lieutenant held. "Some of the photos on those other jars looked familiar. You may find a connection between these two cases."

"I was already thinking the same thing," Foster confirmed. "I'm worried sick about what this is going to do to my town." He shook his head again. "God almighty, I don't know how I could have missed all this."

"Obviously, these people have gone to great lengths to cover their tracks." A clang from her cell phone startled Jess. She'd forgotten to silence it. "Excuse me." She fished it from her bag to mute the annoying sound, but the name on the screen was one she couldn't ignore. "I need to take this call, Sheriff. Please keep me posted on your investigation."

Foster assured her he would keep her up to date. Jess thanked him and headed for the building's front entrance. She hit *call back* without listening to the message Gant had left. Hayes hurried out ahead of her, surveyed the parking lot, and then moved aside for her to exit.

When Gant's voice echoed across the line, she stopped, suddenly unable to make another step and have this conversation. The call was no doubt about Spears. "Sorry. I was in an interview."

"I spoke to Burnett and Black with an update."

Somehow, Jess made it the final few steps to the car. She opened the door and sat down, immediately engulfed by the buildup of heat inside the vehicle. Hayes started the engine and turned the AC to maximum, but it would be a few minutes before it was anything less than stifling inside. She kept her door open to prevent suffocating.

"I'm listening." If he'd thought it was so important to give her the update personally, why the sudden silence?

Because it's bad, Jess.

"We've identified the third woman who went missing."

She waffled between being glad they'd learned her identity and feeling sad for the family who likely now understood how very dire the situation was. With all they didn't know, Jess was certain of one thing: Rory Stinnet and Monica Atmore were in Birmingham. Amanda had basically confirmed that theory. Victim number three would be with them. She'd passed the information to Gant yesterday.

"Lisa Knowles, twenty-three, from Decatur, Alabama."

"She's probably in Birmingham with the other two." Jess got out of the car. She couldn't sit another second. "Is your special Joint Task Force broadening the search in the Birmingham area? Did you even listen to what I told you Amanda said?"

"You know it's not that simple, Jess. A two-hour radius around Scottsboro encompasses far more than Birmingham. It goes without saying that we've broadened our search, particularly in the Birmingham area. You know how this works."

Maybe she did. Before she let her emotions take the lead, she filled him in on the Eli Mooney discovery and what she'd learned from the retired coroner.

"We'll be taking over that scene as well," Gant said, "including the evidence you have in your custody."

"I need a sample for analysis first." She stood her ground. She wasn't wading through the Bureau's red tape to know one way or the other about the fetus. God, she had to talk to Lil. How did she tell her something like this?

What was the point until she knew for certain exactly what they had? She recognized that excuse was getting old. She couldn't continue keeping her sister in the dark about this.

"He's moving faster now, Jess," Gant said, drawing her attention back to the call. "He's growing bolder. My instinct says he's feeling the pressure to bring on the finale. You need to be extremely careful."

"What else would I be?" She might have had a reputation in the past for taking risks, but she had other considerations now. "If that's all you've got, I have things to do, Gant." Before she did anything else, she needed to talk to Dan.

"It's no longer that simple, Jess. Your family and your past being dragged more deeply into this has changed everything."

"What the hell does that mean?" She settled in the seat and closed the car door now that the vents were circulating cold air. "He's been dragging my family into this for weeks." She opted not to ask if Gant had been asleep the past month or so.

"Jess, he's gone from targeting people close to your family and points of interest from your family's past to focusing *only* on your family. The escalating pattern is hard to miss. I've discussed this at length with Chief Black, and we've decided it's best if you have no further involvement in our investigation."

"I don't answer to you or to Chief Black." Fury whipped through her.

"That may be true but, as of this moment, you will not return to the Brownfield farm or the Mooney crime scene. No more talking to Amanda Brownfield. You're out of this, Jess."

She choked on a laugh. "You can't do that, Gant. This is about me. You can't remove me from the investigation."

"I just did. Focus on staying safe, Jess. Spears wants you vulnerable. Don't give him what he wants."

"If I'm off the case," Jess held her breath, "then I guess we have nothing else to discuss." She ended the call.

What in the world did she do now?

"I take it that didn't go well."

"Not at all, Lieutenant. Not at all." Jess reached for her seatbelt. "I need to see Maddie Brownfield."

Hayes shifted into drive. "Heading there now."

Gant hadn't told her she couldn't see Maddie again. He probably hadn't thought it was necessary. Being off the case, by default, included Maddie.

"While I talk to Maddie, I'd like you to take the… evidence by Dr. Baron's office for a DNA sample. Then turn it over to the lab."

"No can do, Chief."

Jess took a moment to get her emotions under control. When she trusted herself to speak without biting his head off, she said calmly. "All right then. Call Dr. Baron and ask if she will wait for us at her office."

"That, I can do."

Jess leaned back in her seat and closed her eyes. How did she get around Gant?

CHAPTER ELEVEN

Jess pushed the swing and four-year-old Maddie Brownfield squealed with delight as she soared ever higher. Hearing her laughter relaxed Jess somehow. Or maybe it was more about how such a simple act made the little girl so happy when her whole life had fallen down around her.

What a shame most adults, including Jess, couldn't appreciate the little things in a time of crisis.

The people who were supposed to protect Maddie had failed. With every part of her being, Jess wanted to protect her child. If somehow she failed, Dan would not. As much as his mother had annoyed Jess at times, she and Dan's father would—until they took their last breaths—be the kind of support system for their child that was missing in Maddie's life.

Jess had an enormous task in front of her. She had to stop Spears. There was no other way to protect the people she loved and the innocent victims he would continue to devastate…like Maddie.

During the drive from Scottsboro, Jess had come to terms with how to handle Gant's decision. She'd go around him. She'd done it before. He wouldn't like it. Chances were he would probably expect her to attempt something along those lines. The only difficult part would be seeing to it that her team stayed out of trouble. If Dan ended up on administrative leave, Black would, in all likelihood, be selected as acting chief. He could make life miserable for Jess and her team. If that happened…

No need to borrow trouble. All her energies had to be centered on ending this game once and for all.

Maddie hopped off the swing, grabbed Jess by the hand, and dragged her over to sit in the grass. The child who wouldn't say a word a few days ago suddenly couldn't stop talking. She went on and on about her new doll named Jess. Emotion almost got the best of her as the little girl explained how Jess was the best doll in the world. Eventually, she stopped chattering to explore the grass for four-leaf clovers.

It was amazing how a child would open up when she felt safe. The people here had made Maddie feel safe with a warm and loving environment. The backyard was fully enclosed with a privacy fence. Surveillance cameras monitored the property and its boundaries. Though it was a shame all that technology and security were necessary, Jess was grateful to see it in place. At some point, permanent arrangements would have to be made. What happened next was up to the court.

"I saw your mom today," Jess told the little girl. No matter that Maddie hadn't mentioned her mother and seemed perfectly happy here with kind strangers, deep down she had to be afraid. The child was four years old. Her mother and grandmother had been her only caretakers until now. Of course, she missed them and wondered where they were even if a part of her—perhaps the part that had seen and heard far more than a small child should—pretended not to notice. She might feel relieved in some way, too.

Maddie jumped up. "I want fireflies!" She rushed to the nearest tree, looked all around it before moving on to a bush.

Jess wasn't going to push her to talk. The psychiatrist assigned to her case had that responsibility.

For a while longer, Jess watched Maddie romp around the yard in search of the elusive fireflies. It wasn't quite dark enough for them to come out. Which reminded Jess, as enjoyable as this visit was, it was time to go. Sylvia was waiting for her.

After rounding up Maddie and ushering her toward the patio, Jess promised, "I'll come see you again soon."

"I made you a pit'chure," Maddie announced as they entered the kitchen.

She released Jess's hand and skipped away. Jess smiled. Watching Maddie made her feel more relaxed than she had in weeks. Was that more of those pregnancy hormones? Did children become more desirable to women who were expecting? Whatever the case, Jess was glad for it.

"She's a lovely child."

Jess turned to the woman who was orchestrating the pots and pans on the stovetop. Whatever they were having for dinner, it smelled incredible. Nicole Green was clearly a multi-talented woman with endless patience.

"She is," Jess agreed.

"The last three days she's been like a flower opening to the sun," Nicole added, smiling. "I've enjoyed being a part of the transition. You'd never know anything bad had happened if not for the nightmares she has every single night."

All those warm, fuzzy feelings Jess had experienced moments ago disappeared. The nightmares would haunt Maddie on some level for the rest of her life. There were so many more transitions to come for this child.

"There's a hearing next Friday," Nicole was saying, drawing Jess from the worrisome thoughts. "The first step in the process of settling Maddie in a home. There are no remaining relatives to reach out to so…"

Maddie reappeared, ending the discussion. Nicole didn't need to say the rest. Jess knew what would happen next.

"For you." Maddie held another masterpiece she'd made. "I 'membered him in my dream."

Puzzled, Jess studied the drawing. A black box of a car with wheels that weren't so round filled the center of the green construction paper. Next to the car was a stick figure with strands of black hair. Jess crouched down to Maddie's eye level. "I'm not sure I know him."

Maddie held the drawing closer to Jess as if she needed to have a better look. "He gived Mommy pit'chures of you."

Black car...? *Someone with pictures.* Flashes of memory—looking in her rearview mirror and seeing that gun aimed at her, finding the flowers on Lori's car, him watching from a distance over and over again, Dan receiving packets of photos. *The dark-haired man.* The same man who'd picked up Amanda at that club and taken her to Spears. The same one Amanda had sworn she didn't know.

"Maybe if you tell me his name I'll remember him."

Maddie shrugged, looked uncertain. "I can't member."

"It doesn't matter." Jess smiled, forcing away the visible tension. "So I can keep this?"

The uncertainty vanished and the little girl nodded enthusiastically.

"Thank you, Maddie."

Maddie walked Jess to the door. When they'd exchanged goodbyes and Jess was out the door, she felt bereft. Finding good parents for Maddie would be crucial. Someone who could look beyond her past.

Someone who would love and cherish her rather than send her away like they had Jess and Lil...over and over.

JEFFERSON COUNTY CORONER'S OFFICE,
7:45 P.M.

Jess wanted to kick something. Gant would not see reason. She'd wanted to see Amanda again to press her about the dark-haired man and Eli Mooney. Gant adamantly refused to allow her access. Gant had insisted that Chief Black would question her tomorrow.

And he would get nothing. Dammit.

"I'll take it from here, Lieutenant Hayes," Sylvia announced as she stripped off her gloves.

Hayes exchanged a look with Jess who was as confused as he was, but then she'd been preoccupied.

Sylvia stripped off the paper lab coat. "I've taken the specimen I need, Lieutenant. You can turn the rest over to BPD's evidence lab. I'm taking Chief Harris home."

"I can ride to the lab with Hayes and then home," Jess suggested. She wanted this day to be over. Two people had been murdered. God only knew if the fetus had really come from her mother. Maddie's hearing was coming up. Gant was trying to close her out of the investigation. To top it all off, she still hadn't heard from Buddy. Every time she called his cell, it went to voicemail. Surely, he'd connected with McPherson by now. Why hadn't he given Jess an update?

"Dr. Baron, I'm—" Hayes began.

"Goodnight, Lieutenant." Baron stood her ground.

Enough. "Go, Lieutenant," Jess ordered, letting him off the hook. "I'll be safe with Dr. Baron."

The door to the autopsy room opened. "Am I late?"

Gina Coleman. What was going on here? This was beginning to look like a setup.

"See, Lieutenant," Sylvia said smugly, "I even have backup."

Hayes held his hands palms out. "I can see I'm outnumbered. So," he gave a little salute, "good-night, ladies."

The door closed behind the lieutenant and Jess sighed. She'd really wanted to go home to Dan. They had a lot to talk about.

"Mmm-hmm," Gina hummed. "I may prefer women, but that guy is *hot.*"

Sylvia shook her head as she peeled off her lab coat. "Too cocky for me. I've come to appreciate the more pliable of the species."

"What's going on, ladies?" Might as well get down to business. These two had something up their sleeves and Jess was, apparently, going to be an accomplice.

Gina, looking sleek and fashionable in a chic gold pantsuit that accentuated her dark looks, and Sylvia, the image of sophistication in her mint skirt and blouse, crossed their arms simultaneously. Jess had a bad feeling she was not going to like this.

"Katherine told us," Sylvia announced.

Jess stopped the mental rant that automatically kicked off whenever Katherine, bless her heart, got on her nerves. She refused to allow anything the woman did or said to upset her ever again. She would have a good relationship with Dan's mother if it killed her.

"Your secret is safe with us," Gina assured her. "We won't tell anyone."

"You could have told us," Sylvia countered. "Then again, I can see why you wouldn't. At your age being knocked up is—"

"Hey," Gina growled. "Be nice."

For a couple of seconds the whole situation felt surreal. Here she was, with one of Dan's ex-lovers and the sister of his second ex-wife. Jess would have laughed except she was too exhausted physically and emotionally. Whatever else these women were, they were her friends.

"At any rate," Sylvia said, "we've decided that, all things considered, you need an intervention."

Jess did laugh then. "I'm afraid you're a little late."

Sylvia rolled her eyes. "Obviously, you're far too focused on work to go shopping. You've been wearing the same four or five suits over and over for weeks."

One, two, three, four...Jess inhaled a deep breath. "It's true. I've been a little busy. By the time I'm through for the day most things are closed and I'm completely exhausted."

"I hear you," Gina tossed in. "The only available options at night are the malls. I hate the malls. That's what tonight is about. We have friends who accommodate our busy schedules."

The one time Jess had gone shopping since moving back to Birmingham was with Dan in a similar outing right after her room at the Howard Johnson and all her things were destroyed. A friend of his mother who owned a designer shop had opened up after hours for them. Felt like a lifetime ago.

"I should call Dan." Jess was late as it was and she really wanted to hear his voice.

"Already done." Sylvia reached for her purse and her keys. "I hope you brought your credit card, Harris."

Jess produced a smile. "I guess we're going shopping."

With Sylvia on one side and Gina on the other, they were off.

"So what does it feel like?"

Startled by the question, Jess considered the best way to answer Gina's question. "Mostly it's exhausting and…a little terrifying."

"She's going to feel fat," Sylvia warned. "Fat and unattractive and used."

Jess felt confident she should have a counter for that, but she wasn't so sure Sylvia was entirely wrong.

"Then the kid will be born and everything will change," Sylvia continued as if she'd had several of her own when she hadn't produced the first child. Sylvia stopped and faced Jess. "This child will become your world. He or she will complete you in a way you won't be able to explain." Sylvia grinned. "Then you'll hate all your friends who still have their figures and their freedom."

"How would you know?" Gina demanded.

"Thank you," Jess said to Gina.

"My ex's second wife told me."

"Not to speak ill of the dead," Jess had solved the poor woman's murder, "why would she say something like that to you?" After all, she had stolen Sylvia's husband of ten years, and then produced the first and only child for said husband.

Sylvia shrugged. "I asked. She gave my husband the one thing I refused to give him. I wanted to know what the big deal was."

A comfortable silence settled around them after Sylvia's odd announcement. They were all three just a little damaged and different. Maybe that was the reason they were so good at their work and made such good friends.

Jess had decided that a woman needed good friends.

THE JUICE, 10:30 P.M.

Jess could hardly keep her eyes open. Too many designer bags to count filled the trunk of Sylvia's Lexus. Jess was now ready for the next couple of months. They had dined on salads with vitamins and nutrient filled juice smoothies with no dessert, unless you counted the organic sweet potato chips.

If she were lucky there was chocolate at home. She would need some before this night was over. She had to admit the evening had been interesting. Besides gaining a new wardrobe, she'd learned that the trial date for Gina's sister had been set.

According to Gina, Juliette's attorney believed she would be sentenced to probation for her part in the death of a fellow graduating high school senior ten years earlier. Contrary to popular thinking, tragedy struck the lives of the wealthy the same as it did everyone else.

Jess had spent the past hour spilling her guts to these two women. Maybe there was something in the juice, she couldn't be sure. Whatever the case, she'd told them about the photo of her father, about Amanda, and the message from Spears. And, then she'd shared the details about the...fetus. Jess closed her eyes. Not simply a fetus, a *baby*. Spears was insinuating her mother had been pregnant when she died.

There had never been any doubt in her mind that he would use her pregnancy against her if he found out. Dammit. How the hell had he found out?

"Today was tough," Sylvia announced. "I'll have some answers for you as quickly as possible."

"I really appreciate it."

Gina glanced around. The small cafe was mostly empty. "I've been talking to my contacts."

Jess leaned toward her, uncaring that Sylvia obviously knew already that Jess had asked Gina for help. "And?"

"Mayor Pratt is spearheading the anti-Dan campaign. He's been calling in all his markers with the city council and prodding the movers and shakers in Birmingham. He wants Dan out. Now."

Jess sagged back against her seat. "We've pretty much established the mayor's motives already."

"What about Dority?" Sylvia asked. "How does she fit into this?"

"Dan and I haven't figured that one out yet," Jess admitted.

Gina leaned forward and spoke for their ears only. "I tried to interview Meredith Dority. She won't talk to me. She won't talk to anyone."

"Daddy spoke to Joe," Sylvia assured Jess. "He warned him that he'd better be able to back up whatever he starts or he would wish he'd never set this nasty business in motion. Joe Pratt didn't reach the office of mayor alone. Daddy cautioned him to remember that."

Emotion tightening around her again, Jess greatly appreciated Dan's friends—her friends—helping. "Dority coming forward now, after all these years reeks of coercion."

"My guess is," Gina confided, "Pratt has something on her. He's bound to have something. She was his assistant for fifteen years."

Sylvia made a derisive sound. "That's what we do—most of us anyway. Those with power keep secrets, particularly about those we might one day need. We watch for missteps so we can use those mistakes to our advantage. It's ugly, but to some power is all that's important."

"I'm staying on Dority," Gina promised. "I will get the truth out of her or, at the very least, a story."

Good reporters were relentless and Gina was the best.

By the time the ladies were ready to call it a night, the shopping spree had made a sizeable dent in Jess's credit card. Though she'd enjoyed the company and actually had a nice time, she needed to see Dan.

Outside the café, Sylvia hit the key fob disarming the security system on her car and unlocking the doors. A BPD cruiser waited behind the Lexus. For the first time since this started, Jess was acutely aware of how much she appreciated the backup.

As they walked the short distance down the block to the parked car, Jess thought of all the times she and Dan, as teenagers, had strolled this street. Coffee shops and martini bars were all the rage now. Back then, the establishments hadn't been quite so sophisticated. Dance clubs and pool halls had dotted the blocks.

"Do you have a due date?" Sylvia wanted to know.

"April twentieth."

"We'll have to plan a baby shower," Gina said with the smile that captivated her audience on a regular basis.

Jess laughed. "I think maybe the wedding should come first."

"Don't be old-fashioned." Sylvia blew off the idea. "Just because you and Dan aren't married yet doesn't mean we can't celebrate the fact that you're pregnant. That's a big deal." She made a face. "In fact, it's a huge deal."

"I certainly didn't have a baby penciled in on my calendar," Jess admitted. "We still have to figure out the house situation."

"I know a really good realtor," Gina said.

"I think Dan and his mother have the—"

"Are you all right?"

A man's voice had all three women looking behind them.

Meredith Dority and a man Jess didn't recognize had exited the Bean House coffee shop. Dority stared at Jess, her face horror-stricken. To Jess's knowledge she'd never met the woman in person.

The man looked from Dority to Jess and back. "We should go, Meredith."

Meredith shook her head, her attention still fixed on Jess.

"Let's go, ladies," Sylvia suggested.

Jess wanted to. She really did, but something about the way Dority stared at her kept her feet glued to the ground.

"I didn't know," Dority pleaded as if asking for Jess's forgiveness.

Her friend or boyfriend, whatever he was, took Dority by the arm and started urging her in the other direction. "Don't say anything else, Meredith."

"The truth would be nice," Gina called out behind the two.

Dority glanced back one last time as the man Jess now presumed to be her attorney steered her away. The pain on her face was something Jess wouldn't soon forget. Meredith Dority hadn't known that Jess was pregnant. Of course, she hadn't. Hardly anyone did. Learning that news had distressed her somehow.

There was only one motive for that sort of reaction...*guilt.*

Dan hauled the last of the shopping bags inside and locked up. "Sylvia said to tell you goodnight." He armed the security system.

"Umm-hmm." For a moment, Jess stared at him. He'd met her at Sylvia's car wearing nothing but those old sweatpants that hung low on his hips. As ready to collapse as she was, she could stand here all night and do nothing except look at him. Her feet argued the point. She kicked off her shoes and sighed at the sheer bliss of feeling the cool floor beneath her aching feet.

Dan pulled her into his arms and held her close. "Tell me about what happened in Scottsboro."

She didn't ask what he'd heard already and who'd told him, she closed her eyes and laid her head against his chest. If only she could forget today. Sylvia and Gina had kept her distracted for a while, but now the horrifying discoveries of the day were back, taunting her.

"For one thing Gant exiled me from the Spears investigation." It wasn't the first time her former boss had kicked her off the case, but that didn't make her like it this time any better than she had the last time. A big breath shuddered out of her. "Sheriff Foster located the owner of the car Spears used to send me a message."

She told him about Mooney and his shop of horrors. Keeping her emotions at bay proved particularly difficult as she shared the part about the baby in the jar and how her mother may have been pregnant making the child—a boy—her brother. Confounded tears rolled down her cheeks anyway. She couldn't hope to stop them.

Before she realized he'd moved, Dan swooped her up into his arms. "Enough talking. I'm taking you to bed."

Dan settled her onto her feet next to the bed and began removing her clothes. He kissed her tears away. She'd never in her life been so emotional. This pregnancy was turning her into a blubbering fool.

She opened her mouth to apologize for falling apart, but all she could do was stare at the gorgeous man attending to her so gently. His muscled chest and strong arms made her ache desperately for him.

"Make love to me, Dan."

He kissed her tenderly. She closed her eyes and lost herself to the feel of his hands moving over her body. One by one, he released the buttons of her jacket and slipped it off. His arms went around her waist and he unfastened her skirt. It fell to the floor. His fingers slipped beneath the catch of her bra and liberated her from the binding satin. He dropped to his knees, his palms sliding down her torso. She shivered as his fingers tugged her panties down her thighs.

He kissed her belly and she gasped.

Lifting her into his arms once more, he kissed her so softly, over and over. He lowered her to the bed and came down on top of her. The weight of him had her body moving restlessly and she forgot all about being tired.

He made love to her slowly, whispering sweet words to her until they were both gasping for breath and clinging helplessly to each other.

When their breathing had quieted, she held him tightly and told him about running into Meredith. Jess felt the tension in his body, and she wished she could make it go away.

She wished all of this would just go away.

CHAPTER TWELVE

Jess stared at her reflection. The dress was sleeve-less and formfitting from bust to waist then flared into a loose pleated skirt. Gina had raved about the sapphire color brightening Jess's pale complexion. Sylvia, on the other hand, had pointed out how the flared skirt and the matching three-quarter sleeve cardigan would help camouflage subtle weight gains.

Then there were the shoes. Jess cringed a little when she looked at her new shiny black shoes. They were the Mary Jane style she loved but with only two-inch, sturdy heels. *Shoes for the woman on the go*, that was what the label on the box said. The look of classic pumps, the shop owner had lauded, with the feel and sensibility of running shoes. The extra cush-ioning inside felt nice to Jess's feet, but the pumps looked like old lady shoes.

This was precisely why she had always shopped alone. Who knew having friends could be so painful to the ego? She surveyed the dozen new dresses and suits hanging in her closet. Or so damaging to the credit card?

Dan came up behind her. His arms went around her waist and he leaned down to kiss her cheek. "You look amazing."

Jess lifted one foot and twisted it side to side. "You like my old lady shoes?"

"I find them sexy as hell." He slid one hand over her belly. "Everything about you is sexy as hell."

Jess turned in his arms and searched his face. She still winced a little each time she looked at the small bandage. "You might not like what I'm about to do."

A smile slid across that tempting mouth. "Do I ever when it comes to work?"

She sighed. "I need to know how all this connects to my parents." Jess shook her head. "And Maddie. I have to make sure she's okay. If Lil and I are related to her that gives us legal grounds to protect her."

He gave a somber nod. "You do what you have to do as long as you take all the necessary precautions to protect *you*."

Jess reached up and touched his forehead, careful of the bandage. "I'm glad you're not trying to put me under house arrest."

"You need the truth." He caressed her cheek with the pad of his thumb. "I understand."

She hugged him hard. "You deserve the truth, too. I can't believe we ran into Dority last night." Jess thought about the horrified look on the other woman's face. She drew back and met Dan's expectant gaze. "But I'm glad we did. She's hiding something, Dan. Guilt was written all over her face. What does Pratt have on her?"

"I don't know." A frown tugged at his lips. "Whatever it is, she won't return my phone calls."

"If Pratt wants you out so badly, why doesn't he just fire you?" As the mayor, the old coot had the power to select as well as to dismiss a chief of police. Jess reached up and adjusted Dan's collar.

"There would be repercussions for him and he knows it. The city council and most of the power in the city are people who've known me my whole life." He reached for his jacket and slipped it on. "He's walking a tight rope."

Jess chewed her lip. "He turned on you when you stopped listening to his suggestions. About me."

"He was wrong, Jess."

"Still." She searched his eyes for any sign of regret. "This started with me."

"It ends with me," Dan said firmly. "If this city doesn't stand behind me, then I don't want to be chief of police, but I believe they will."

To see that determination and confidence made her smile. "I'm certain they will."

He pulled her back into his arms. "I'm glad you're not angry with my mother for telling Sylvia and Gina about the baby."

"She's excited. How can I hold that against her?" Jess had made up her mind about Katherine. From now on, she was keeping Katherine's good points front and center. A woman who could raise a man like Dan undoubtedly had many good points beneath that need for a certain image.

The clang of her phone echoed. Jess made a face. "And it begins."

Dan released her. "Go be deputy chief. I have to find my blue tie."

Jess hurried to the kitchen counter. "It's hanging on the back of the bathroom door." She unplugged her phone from the charger and accepted the call she'd been waiting for. "Did you get lost, Corlew?"

Buddy chuckled. "So it's Corlew this morning, is it?"

"Considering I called you several times yesterday and you never called me back, you're on my bad side this morning. Did you talk to McPherson?"

"You bet. And I talked real fast cause he had a gun to my head."

Jess cringed. "Do I want to know how that happened?"

"Probably not. Anyway, it worked out and he had an interesting theory about the Brownfields and your father—for what it's worth. Based on what he told me, I think we should talk to Wanda. Can you arrange that?"

"Of course. What did he tell you?"

"McPherson claims he knew your father, Jess. He doesn't believe Lee was part of what the Brownfields were doing. He says this is a setup of some kind."

Jess leaned heavily against the counter and willed her heart to slow its pounding. "Does he have any evidence? Did he know my father that well?"

"That's all he was willing to say, but I saw photos of him with your family. He definitely knew them. He booted me off his property with a strong warning not to come back. I'd already had a look around and found nothing in the house. He has an office of sorts in a building out back, but there was nothing related to the case other than those photos. If he has any kind of proof of whatever he knows, he plans to keep it to himself."

"Did you get the impression he was telling the truth?" There was never a doubt in her mind that he knew plenty. What reason could he have for refusing to cooperate other than the fear of exposing his own actions?

"Yeah," Buddy confirmed. "I believe what he said about your father is the truth. I also think there's probably a hell of a lot he's not telling."

"All right. I'll set it up with Wanda and call you back."

"Make it soon," he recommended.

"Definitely." Jess ended the call and reached for the glass of water she'd left by the sink. Her throat felt suddenly too dry.

Was it possible that her father was nothing more than a cheater? The concept was a bit more palatable than the thought that he might be a murderer... but it all felt wrong.

What happened to the idyllic childhood she remembered?

"You okay?"

Jess turned in time to watch Dan adjust his tie. She wanted their child to have a normal, happy childhood. She wanted a happy, normal life with Dan. If all that she remembered was a lie, how could she trust anything to be real, much less normal?

There was one thing she knew with complete certainty: she could trust Dan. No matter what else happened, that truth was unshakable.

Summoning her determination, she mustered up a smile for him. "I am, yes. That was Buddy. He wants to meet with Wanda to go over some things he learned from the ABI guy who claims my father was setup somehow."

Dan tugged at a strand of her hair. "You need me there?"

"You have enough fires to put out without me dragging you into the ones blazing around me."

"Your fires are my fires." He kissed her cheek. "Hayes is here, by the way."

Jess frowned at the idea Hayes took it upon himself to decide who would be her ride today. "I didn't call anyone yet. I swear that man gets on my last nerve some days."

"I asked him to come by early," Dan explained. "I thought since you were with him yesterday you would be today, and I have to leave for the office earlier than usual."

"In that case, I won't chew him out." She gave Dan a peck on the lips. "You be careful, too. I'm not the only one Spears has his sights on."

When Dan was out the door, Jess made the call to Wanda. Her aunt was happy to help in any way she could. Jess should appreciate her attitude more but forgiving Wanda was a work in progress.

Her next call was to Sheriff Roy Griggs. The Jefferson County sheriff was about to provide her with a way around Supervisory Special Agent Gant.

DRUID HILLS, 10:00 A.M.

Wanda Newsom sat in her well-worn chair, hands clasped in her lap. While Buddy chatted with her about days gone by, Jess studied the woman. Gray had overtaken Wanda's blond hair. A few fleeting strands of the honey color she had shared with her sister remained. Both Wanda and Helen had brown eyes, just like Jess and Lil. Despite having no real desire to acknowledge it, Wanda and Jess's mother looked as much alike as Jess and Lil did, but the two women couldn't have been more different.

Helen Harris had been a devoted wife and mother. Wanda had practically lost her mind when, at age twenty-two, her husband, Johnny Paul Newsom, was killed while advising on a military operation. She'd chosen to drown her sorrows in alcohol and zone out on drugs rather than deal with the reality of life and loss.

Wanda's decision had been her own until Jess and Lil's parents died. Then, the childless widow had suddenly become the caretaker of two little girls. Rather than meet the challenge, she'd stuck with the drugs, the booze, and the bringing johns home with Jess and Lil in the next room.

Jess doubted she would ever be able to forgive Wanda completely for her part in casting two kids into the foster care system, but at Lil's urging she was trying. After all, Wanda had found God and professed she was a Christian now. Who was Jess to pass judgment?

"We'd like to have a look at whatever family photos you have that belonged to Lee and Helen," Buddy was saying now.

Wanda got to her feet. "I'll get them for you. Would you like coffee or tea?" She gazed at Jess hopefully.

Jess shook her head. "Do you recall my mother ever mentioning anything at all about my father's work?"

Wanda blinked, her hopeful expression falling. "We really didn't talk about Lee's work. We were—"

"Estranged," Jess finished for her. "That's right. My mother didn't agree with your lifestyle at the time."

Wanda lowered her gaze. "She wanted to protect you girls from me. I can't blame her. Years later, I tried to see her. She refused. That time it was because of your father's associates, but she wouldn't give me any details."

Hard as it was, Jess set aside her personal feelings and said what needed to be said. "She would be very proud of you now."

The emotion that danced across Wanda's face moved Jess. She didn't want to feel anything toward this woman but there it was.

"Thank you, Jessie Lee. I hope so."

Wanda disappeared down the narrow hall of her small home. Jess closed her eyes and attempted to block the flood of bad memories associated with this place.

"That was nice of you to say, Jess."

She opened her eyes and met Buddy's. "I just hope we're not wasting our time."

Wanda reappeared with a shoebox. "This is everything I have." She handed the box over to Jess. "Keep it as long as you like. I hope you find something that helps."

Jess stared at the box. "This is it?" Her parents' lives had been culled down to nothing more than a shoebox. How could that be?

"That's everything," Wanda said, her head down again.

Oh hell. There she went, being insensitive again. "Thank you." Jess took a breath. "I appreciate you taking care of these all this time."

Wanda nodded. "I wish I'd done better."

"This will help," Jess assured her.

She and Buddy sifted through the pile of old photos. He teased Jess from time to time about the ones that included her. The talk and the teasing lapsed when they encountered a photo at what appeared to be a family gathering.

"Where was this taken?" Jess offered the photo to Wanda.

Rather than take it she moved to the sofa and sat down beside Jess. "That was at the Irondale house where your mom and dad lived with you kids." She pointed to something in the background. "Remember the swing set?"

The swing set was still there. Jess had seen the old rusted out thing last week.

"Your mom and dad had a big Fourth of July cookout that year."

Jess turned the photo over and found the date written on the back. "That was a couple weeks before the accident."

Wanda nodded. "I wasn't there since they didn't want me around, but I tried to salvage all the photos I could."

"What do you mean salvage? Weren't you the one who packed up their belongings?"

"Yes, but there was a robbery sometime after the accident."

Jess glanced at Buddy. "At the house?"

Wanda fidgeted with the hem of her skirt. "It was a few days before I went back there. I had the funeral to arrange and you two girls to take care of." She shrugged. "I guess it was four or five days after the funeral. I went to the house and someone had broken in. The place was a mess."

"So you don't know any of these people?" Jess asked, moving on. She would find out what she could about the break in later. Surely there was a police report.

Wanda shook her head. "Just Helen and Lee and Reverend Henshaw."

Jess stared at the group gathered in what was her childhood backyard. Several she recognized immediately. Reverend Henshaw. Randall McPherson. Her parents, of course, but there were three other faces she didn't recognize. The reverend she could understand being invited to a family barbecue, but McPherson? Buddy had told her about the photos he'd seen in McPherson's shed-turned-office. Clearly, the retired ABI agent had known her parents better than he'd wanted to admit to Jess. Did this mean he was telling the truth about her father?

Every time she thought she was getting closer to answers, she found more questions.

Her cell rang. She passed the photo to Buddy and dug for her phone. *Harper.* "What's going on, Sergeant?"

"Chief, we found where Henshaw has been staying. I think you need to see this before we call for the evidence techs. We're downtown at one of the old hotels, the Redmont, on Fifth Avenue."

"I'm on my way, Sergeant."

"FYI," Harper alerted, "Cook and Wells are headed back from Scottsboro. Agent Manning asked them to leave the scene since SPU isn't on the case anymore. Chief Black backed him up."

Jess smiled. The Bureau and Chief Black were in for a surprise. "We'll rendezvous at your location, Sergeant. We can discuss that issue then." Jess ended the call and put her phone away.

Buddy was busy snapping pics of some of the old photographs with his cell.

"Do you mind if I borrow these for a while? I'll have copies made." Jess needed more time with the photos. She wanted to show them to Lily.

"Keep them," Wanda said. "They really belong to you and Lil."

"Thank you." Jess couldn't think of anything else to add. She supposed there was plenty that needed to be said at some point.

When Buddy had finished, Jess accepted the shoebox of photos and moved toward the door. "I appreciate your help. If you think of anything else, please let me know."

Wanda shuffled along behind her. "I will." She smiled at Buddy. "I'm glad I got to see you again, Mr. Corlew."

"Buddy," he insisted. "You feel free to call me anytime as well, Ms. Newsom."

Hayes was out of his car and headed toward Jess before she was down the steps. He'd opted to stay outside to make some calls. Jess hoped she would eventually find her way past being suspicious of his motives. Since the business in Scottsboro when he'd followed her and Lori as if they weren't capable of getting the job done or taking care of themselves, she hadn't been able to see him in the same light.

"Chief Black is trying to reach you." Hayes waved his cell. "He said he'd called yours twice already."

"I was in a meeting," Jess said. "Did you tell him that?"

"I did. He wants to meet with you as soon as you're available."

"In that case, how about next week?" Jess turned to Buddy. "Harper located where Henshaw has been staying. I'll let you know if we find anything useful."

"I'm going to see Amanda." Buddy shrugged. "See what she'll tell me."

Jess gave him a skeptical look. Gant had refused her access last night. "I doubt they'll let you see her."

Buddy grinned. "You forget I have friends in all sorts of places, kid. Getting in won't be a problem."

"I'd like to know why she lied to me about the dark-haired man." She had told Buddy about her visit with Maddie.

"I'll be asking her that one for sure."

"I expect a phone call immediately after you've spoken with her," Jess ordered.

"You're the boss."

Her cell started that confounded racket again as she watched Buddy drive away. *Gina.* Jess's pulse bounced into a faster rhythm. "Tell me you have something new?"

Pause. "I take it Dan hasn't reached you."

Jess started moving toward Hayes's car. Harper was waiting. "About?"

"Meredith Dority was found dead in her mother's home this morning. My sources say it looks like a homicide."

Oh God. "Thanks, Gina. I should call Dan."

I didn't know. Jess thought of the look of horror on Dority's face last night as she'd uttered those words.

Dan's phone went straight to voicemail. Hearing his voice in the recorded greeting made Jess want to cry.

This nightmare just kept expanding and escalating.

CHAPTER THIRTEEN

"Good morning, Tara." Dan smiled at his reception-ist who was busy with a call. She glanced up at him but the return smile was slow in coming.

He'd been MIA all morning. The decision was a confident move for a man on the verge of losing his job. Dan had enough personal leave time and vacation days saved up to take the next three months off with pay, a couple of hours was nothing. Anyone who needed to reach him knew how.

"Good morning, Chief." Shelia, his secretary, offered him a handful of messages as he reached her desk.

He'd called his secretary half an hour ago to say he was on his way in. He'd missed a call from Jess while he was on the line with Shelia. He'd tried to call her back but he'd gotten her voicemail.

"Let's hope it stays one," Dan replied as he accepted the messages. "Would you get Chief Harris on the line for me, please?"

"Chief Black is waiting in your office." Shelia winced. "I told him you were on your way in."

"That's fine," Dan assured her. "I'll call Chief Harris after Chief Black and I are finished." Shelia and Tara were worried about him as well as their jobs. This was a difficult situation for all of them. "Thanks, Shelia."

At his door, Dan hesitated a moment. He'd supported this city for two decades, dedicated to the goal of making Birmingham a better place. None of that mattered to men like Pratt. Dan had stopped taking the mayor's suggestions on how to run the BPD and suddenly he was the enemy. There had been friction for a couple of years, but the real trouble had started more recently. The mayor might take this position from him, but he couldn't change what Dan had done for the city.

Whatever happened, Jess and the baby were his top priorities now.

With renewed purpose, he opened the door and strode into his office. Harold Black stood behind Dan's desk gazing out his window.

"Like the view?" Dan dropped his briefcase on his desk and waited for the other man to get out of the way.

Harold moved around to the front of the desk and settled into one of the chairs. "I was surprised to find you weren't in your office this morning."

Dan lowered into his chair. "I had personal business. Do you want my secretary to start forwarding you my calendar?"

Harold heaved a sigh. "No need for the hostility, Dan."

Somehow, hostility seemed fitting at the moment. "What is it you want, Harold?"

Harold propped his elbows on the chair arms and steepled his fingers. "Let's start with your whereabouts this morning. According to the officer on Chief Harris's surveillance detail today, you departed the apartment the two of you share around eight. Did you have breakfast with someone?"

Fury shot through Dan. "Whatever it is you have to say, I suggest you move right to the point. I have some catching up to do."

"Meredith Dority is dead, Dan. Murdered."

The fury died instantly. Though their marriage had been a mistake for both of them, they had parted on good terms. Meredith was—had been—a good person, a caring person with whom he'd had a lot in common. After the divorce, they had remained friends, until now.

How could she be dead?

"This morning? What happened?" Dan braced for the painful details.

"You may or may not be aware, but her mother fell and broke her hip three weeks ago. That's the reason Meredith took a leave of absence from her position in Montgomery. She's been helping her mother."

Dan shook his head. "I had no idea." He hadn't heard from Meredith in a long while before last week. They were both busy people, time slipped away.

"Her mother was asleep in her bedroom," Harold explained. "The doorbell woke her. She, of course, requires assistance getting in and out of bed so leaving her room was impossible. She did, however, hear the confrontation. The visitor and Meredith exchanged heated words. Mrs. Dority heard their raised voices, the slamming of the door, and then her daughter crying."

Dan felt ill. "I—"

Harold held up a hand for Dan to wait. "No more than three or four minutes later there was another, quieter discussion. The next thing Mrs. Dority heard was a struggle and then nothing."

Dan couldn't speak for a moment. His entire being ached for the pain Meredith had suffered and for the agony her mother endured not being able to help daughter. "How...?" He couldn't bear to say the rest.

"She was strangled."

Jesus Christ. Who would do this? "Was this a robbery?" The elderly were far too often targets. Under normal circumstances, Mrs. Dority would have been home alone.

Harold stared at him for a long moment before answering. "Nothing from the home was taken."

"Why the hell wasn't I notified? Whatever happens tomorrow or the day after that doesn't matter. Right now," Dan banged his fist against the desk, "I am still the chief of police. Why didn't you call me about this?"

He had never required that his division chiefs keep him abreast of their activities day by day as long as he was kept up to date within a reasonable time-frame. He didn't need blow-by-blow accounts. He trusted the people he placed at the highest levels within the department, but this was different. He should have been informed of Meredith's death.

"Dan." Harold's face was grave now. "Mrs. Dority recognized the intruder's voice."

Comprehension hit Dan square in the chest.

"She said the man she heard arguing with her daughter was *you.*" Harold held up both hands when Dan would have butted in. "Before you say anything, I need to advise you that you have the right to remain silent. Anything you say can—"

"I know my rights, by God! Yes, I stopped by to see Meredith this morning." Dan worked at relaxing his tense muscles. *Meredith was dead.* Jesus Christ. He couldn't believe Pratt would have anything to do with this. Spears maybe, but why? "Yes, we argued." What had he been thinking?

"Was she expecting you?"

Dan shook his head. "Jess ran into her last night and Meredith said something that leads me to believe she was being coerced into the accusations she made."

"What did she say to Chief Harris?"

"I guess she overheard Jess sharing our future plans with Sylvia and Gina." Dan refused to share the news about the baby with Harold. "Meredith seemed distraught and said something to the effect that she didn't know. Her companion, a male Jess didn't recognize, urged Meredith not to say more. Meredith and I hadn't spoken since she went public with these ludicrous allegations. I felt it was time we cleared the air."

Harold shifted in his chair. "Are you certain you don't want to call your attorney before we discuss this any further?"

"Are you officially questioning me?"

Harold rubbed at his temple. "Let's call this a pre-interview."

Dan closed his eyes and shook his head. *Unbelievable.*

"What do you want me to do, Dan?" Harold held out his arms in a helpless gesture. "I have no choice. Someone has to do this. If you'd rather I call in someone else, that's what I'll do."

Dan nodded. "You're right. Let's just do this. I arrived at her mother's home around eight-thirty this morning. I never made it past the open doorway. Meredith wouldn't invite me in. She said she couldn't. I asked why and she wouldn't say."

"Did you sense Meredith was afraid of you in any way?"

"Of course not! She kept looking toward the street as if she were afraid someone would see me there."

"When she asked you to leave, did you?"

Dan shook his head. "No. I demanded to know why she'd fabricated these stories about me. She kept repeating that *she had no choice, she had no choice.*

I tried reasoning with her. I offered her police protection. She wouldn't tell me anything. She continued to demand that I leave. She said she couldn't be seen talking to me."

"So she thought someone was watching her?"

"That was my impression."

Harold scrubbed his jaw. "Dan, you must understand how this looks."

"In retrospect going there was a bad idea. Frankly, I'm dumbfounded, Harold. I can't understand why she did this or who would want to hurt her." He exhaled a frustrated breath. "How's her mother?"

"Devastated, as you can imagine."

"I can't have her thinking I did this."

"A neighbor saw your rental car leaving the residence within the timeframe the ME believes the murder occurred."

Holy hell. "Did anyone see who came to the house after me? Meredith was alive when I walked away from her door."

Harold shook his head. "This is bad, Dan. Worse than the business with Allen. The fact that her mother heard you argue with Meredith and then leave only to allegedly return a few minutes later may show premeditation. It's one thing to kill someone in the heat of the moment. It's another one entirely to walk away even for a few minutes and come back to do the deed. You know this as well as I do. The DA will argue that you had sufficient time to calm down before you returned to kill Meredith. That's premeditated murder, Dan."

"I didn't go back, Harold." Fury pounded at Dan again. "I left."

"I, of all people, know you didn't do this. The question is can we prove it?"

"Someone had to see something besides my rental car."

"And if they did, we will find them," Harold assured him. "Right now, there are two things we must do. We have to rule you out based on physical evidence and we have to prove someone else was close enough to swoop in and murder her in the nick of time to frame you."

The whole scenario sounded contrived, yet Dan knew it was true.

"Do what you have to do to rule me out, Harold. I never touched her and she never touched me. She struggled with her attacker, there had to be some sort of evidence exchange."

Harold nodded. "Let's hope that's the case. I'll have a tech come up and take samples for comparison. Meanwhile, I would suggest you call your attorney. The man can't defend you if you don't keep him informed."

"I want to talk to Mrs. Dority." Dan needed her to know he didn't do this.

"Stay away from her for now. Anything you do or say will only send the wrong message."

The intercom buzzed. "Chief," Shelia said, "I'm sorry to interrupt but your mother is on line one. She says it's very important that she speak with you."

Harold stood. "Go ahead. I'll wait outside for the tech to arrive."

"Stay. I don't want anyone suggesting I did away with evidence while you weren't looking."

Harold gave an acknowledging nod as Dan thanked his secretary. He picked up the receiver and pushed the blinking light. "Mom, is everything all right?"

"No, Dan, it absolutely is not. You must talk to your father as soon as possible."

Dan knew from the sound of her voice that nothing too troubling had actually happened. "What's going on with Dad?"

"He refuses to schedule his checkup. You know how important it is that he sees his doctor regularly. With us both worried sick about you, it's crucial that he go. That heart attack almost killed him. I don't want a repeat performance."

"You're right. I'll come by after work today and speak to him."

"You're the only one he listens to," Katherine said, her voice quavering a bit.

"Don't worry. We'll get him in for his checkup. You have my word."

"Thank you, son. I'm counting on you."

Dan gave his mother one last reassurance before ending the call. Katherine had a reputation for overreacting, but this time he wasn't taking any chances.

"Everything all right?"

"I don't know, Harold. I just don't know," Dan confessed. When the news about Meredith hit the media, his parents were going to be devastated.

A knock on his office door signaled the tech had arrived.

"You're sure about this?" Harold asked once more.

"I have nothing to hide." Dan had truth on his side. He hadn't touched Meredith. She was very much alive and in tears when she slammed the door in his face.

And Dan still had no idea why she'd set out to help ruin him.

CHAPTER FOURTEEN

A Birmingham landmark since the early 1920s, the Redmont Hotel had the customary tales of hauntings and mysterious deaths. The classic brick and terra cotta building stood thirteen floors high and sat at the corner of two of downtown's busiest streets.

Jess had only been inside once. At seventeen she'd come with Lil to pick up Wanda. They hadn't seen their aunt in years, but the police had called and said someone had to come pick her up. Wanda had been staying with some guy who'd left her at the hotel wasted on drugs and with two days' rent due. Lil had been so embarrassed. Pooling every nickel they possessed it still wasn't enough to pay the hotel bill. Jess had borrowed the money from her new boyfriend, Dan Burnett. She hadn't told him what she needed the money for and he hadn't asked. When the bill was paid, Wanda had refused to leave the room. She'd been sure her man was coming back. Jess had called Buddy then. He'd sweet-talked Wanda from the room.

Apparently, Jess had completely forgotten the unpleasant episode. No matter that twenty-five years had passed, as soon as she saw the building with its name standing high atop it like a southern version of the Hollywood sign, Jess remembered.

Lieutenant Hayes appeared on the sidewalk near her door, and Jess realized she was still sitting in the car.

Meredith Dority was dead. *Murdered.* Jess hated what she knew Dan was going through right now. Unable to reach him on his cell, she had called the office. His secretary explained that he was in a closed door meeting with Chief Black. Whether the meeting was about Dority or not, Jess doubted anything good for Dan would come of it.

She cleared her head and stepped from the car. She spotted Harper's SUV. No other official vehicles had arrived. At the front entrance, Jess hesitated and turned back to the street. That tingly sensation that warned someone was watching her scaled her spine.

As if the dark-haired man in the picture Maddie had drawn had suddenly come to life, a black Infiniti with heavily tinted windows cruised down Fifth Avenue. Jess didn't need to see the driver, she instinctively knew it was him.

For one instant, she gauged the distance between her and Hayes's car. Could they reach his vehicle in time to follow the Infiniti?

The Infiniti rocketed forward as if she had telegraphed the thought to the driver. Darting between the other cars, the driver made a hard right on Second Avenue and disappeared.

He was watching her again. It was possible he'd never stopped. Either way, he wanted her to know he was close. Gant was right. Spears was feeling the pressure to advance to the finale. Though no one had cornered him, the combined efforts of the Task Force were slowly boxing him in. His time was running out.

He's coming for you, Jessie Lee! Fear shivered through her. She shook it off and strode determinedly toward the hotel entrance.

She might be his end game, but she also intended to be the end of him.

The marble-floored lobby with its soaring ceiling and glittering chandelier led to the elevator. The wait for a car to arrive was long enough for Jess to toy with the idea of climbing six flights of stairs. Thankfully, the elevator doors opened before she made the mistake of suggesting the idea to Hayes. As comfortable as her new shoes were, the idea of that many stairs was not appealing.

On the sixth floor, a narrow carpeted hallway led to room 624. Harper waited at the door. "Good morning, Chief." He glanced at Hayes. "Detective Wells is inside."

"Crime scene techs on the way?" Jess looked beyond Harper through the open door. The room was a wreck. Her heart rate picked up its pace as she slipped on shoe covers.

"No, ma'am. I thought I'd wait and see how you wanted me to handle the request considering Agent Gant removed our team from the investigation."

Jess tugged on a pair of gloves. "We'll take care of that in a bit, Sergeant. Let's see what we have here first."

She entered the hotel room and her lungs were suddenly unable to fill with air. Photos of Jess and handwritten pages were posted on every available inch of wall space. On each page, lines were highlighted in yellow. Scattered on the bed and desk were newspapers—old newspapers. Articles and headlines were circled in red.

In the middle of the room, Jess hesitated. A newspaper photo of her hung above the desk. Surrounding the photo were dozens of clippings about Spears and the other cases she had worked since returning to Birmingham. An iPad lay on the desk. The battery was dead.

"Chief, I think these handwritten pages are from a diary or journal."

Jess dragged her attention from the newspaper clipping to Lori. "Henshaw's?"

"I think," Lori said tentatively, "they were written by your mother. Look at this page."

Pulse accelerating, Jess moved to the wall and studied the first of dozens of pages. She didn't recognize the handwriting, yet her heart seemed to stumble as she read the words.

Lee didn't come home this week. I'm worried. I watch my girls sleep and I fear what the future holds for them. Please, God, help us.

A cold, cold darkness slid through Jess. She reached out, touched the yellowed pages. "Where is…" She cleared the emotion from her throat and turned to Lori. "Where is Officer Cook?"

Lori glanced at the door. "He's taking the detective's exam today."

That news shook Jess from the daze she'd fallen into. "Well…good." She had no idea why she didn't know about that, but she was glad for Cook. Strange that he hadn't asked for her approval first. "Where are Harper and—?"

"Right here, Chief." Harper strode in from the corridor, the lieutenant on his heels.

Jess hadn't heard any raised voices, but she had the distinct impression the two had exchanged unfriendly words. "Sergeant, plug in that iPad and see if the reverend left us anything there." She shifted her attention to Hayes. "Lieutenant, bring in the box of photos I picked up this morning." She turned back to Lori. "Some of the family photos I picked up from my aunt have dates written on the back by my mother. We can compare the writing on those to these pages."

"Sergeant, see if Ricky Vernon can lend us a hand ASAP." Vernon was an evidence tech who had a love for all things electronic. He'd helped Jess before and he was damned good at his job. If there was something on that iPad, he would find it.

"Yes, ma'am."

Jess turned back to Lori. "I'd like photos of all this. I want everything documented by SPU in addition to the documenting the forensic techs will do."

"On it."

Jess moved around the room and studied page after page from the diary apparently kept by her mother. Her heart pounded so fast it threatened to burst. She could hardly breathe. She kept wishing Lil were here. She should see this at some point. Why hadn't they known their mother kept a journal?

A moment was required for her to put aside her emotions and to look at the scene like a cop. The room was in disarray. The reverend, presumably, had written page after page of notes. Most of the pages repeated what he'd found in the journal or simply spouted nonsensical lines. His handwriting had grown increasingly frantic. Numerous references to the Brownfield family and to Spears had been made. Pages from the Bible had been removed and taped to the wall as well. Whatever was going on in Henshaw's mind, either he'd started to lose control or he'd been afraid.

"Vernon is on the way," Harper said as he joined her.

"Did you speak to the hotel manager?" Reverend Henshaw had been MIA for two months. It looked as if he'd been here most of that time.

"I did. Henshaw checked in on July fifteenth. He refused to allow housekeeping in the room. This morning the housekeeper came in anyway. She saw all this and called the manager. One look at the room and he realized the murdered reverend he'd read about in the paper was the man who'd rented this room. He called BPD. Dispatch sent the call our way."

"Have you discovered any documented history of mental illness?"

"No, ma'am. Henshaw underwent a yearly physical with the same doc for the past thirty years. No history of illness, physical or mental. The nurse I spoke with said the man never got sick."

Jess moved back to the photo and articles about her work with the BPD. "If he had something to tell me, why didn't he contact me?"

"Maybe he was searching for an answer before he made contact," Harper suggested.

"Maybe." Jess wished she could have spoken to him. If he knew she was back in town, why didn't he talk to her? Why hadn't he contacted Lil in all these years? Where had this man of God been when two young girls lost their parents and had no decent place to go? Anger lashed through Jess. *Nowhere to be found, that's where.*

Hayes returned with the shoebox of photos. Jess looked through the photos until she found several with handwritten dates on the back. She passed one to Harper and one to Lori.

Jess went to one of the pages she recalled being dated June fourteenth. A photo from the shoebox carried the date January sixteenth. The j's were exactly the same as were the u's. Jess reminded herself to breathe. The dates were definitely written by the same person.

"What's going on here?"

Jess cringed at the sound of Black's voice. She squared her shoulders and prepared for battle. "Stop right there, Chief, this is a crime scene. If you're coming in you need to take the necessary precautions."

Fury tightened the man's face. "I've attempted to reach you several times, Chief Harris. I'd like to speak with you in private."

Jess produced a smile. "Of course." She was prepared for this conversation. She didn't bother closing the door as she joined Black in the corridor. She wanted her team to hear this. "What do you need? I'm a little busy here."

"Correct me if I'm wrong, Harris, but it's my understanding you and your team have been taken off the Spears investigation by Agent Gant."

"That's true," Jess agreed.

He frowned. "Then, why are you here? The Spears investigation encompasses the Henshaw murder as well as the Brownfield murders."

"Oh." Jess laughed. "I'm sorry. I assumed you understood." She reached into her bag and removed the SPU handbook—the very one Black helped compose. She thrust it at him. "Section One, paragraph one. The newly formed Special Problems Unit operates under the authority of the Birmingham Police Department *and* the Jefferson County Sheriff's Department, *equally.* Sheriff Griggs has reopened the cold case involving Lee and Helen Harris, former residents of his county, and he assigned that case to SPU. Since the Henshaw case is related, I'm simply doing my job."

Black smiled patiently. "I'm certain a quick phone call to Sheriff Griggs will clear up the confusion. He must be unaware of Gant's orders and of your connection to the Harrises."

Jess was the one smiling this time. "Why don't I clear up the confusion for you, Chief. The Bureau has no jurisdiction on this cold case unless local law enforcement requests assistance or relinquishes control, Sheriff Griggs isn't doing either, and he is well aware of my personal connection. Now, if we have that all cleared up, I have work to do."

"You're making a mistake, Harris," Black warned. "Your every misstep reflects poorly on Chief Burnett. Are you intent on ruining him?"

"Frankly, I believe you're doing that all by yourself, Chief Black. Do you really want to move up the food chain so badly?"

The words hit their mark. Black was livid. Just when she felt certain he would blast her, he flinched, then reached into his pocket and withdrew his cell phone. "Black."

Jess plucked the handbook from his grasp and tucked it into her bag. He could pull his own copy. A quick phone call to Sheriff Griggs had taken care of her problem with Gant. Griggs was more than happy to help and assured Jess he'd back her up whenever she needed him.

"When?"

The urgency in that solitary word snapped Jess back to attention.

"Issue BOLOs immediately. I'll be right there." Black shoved his phone into his pocket. "If you had anything to do with this, Harris, I will see that you are prosecuted under every applicable federal and state law."

"Everything all right out here, Chief?"

Jess waved Hayes off. "What're you talking about, Black?"

"That was Roark. Amanda Brownfield walked out of the hospital less than twenty minutes after being visited by Buddy Corlew."

For heaven's sake! What was Buddy thinking? Jess abandoned that worry for an even bigger one. "I should warn Nicole Green. Maddie may be in danger."

"Are you saying you had nothing to do with this?" Black demanded.

"Amanda Brownfield is a violent psychopath. A serial killer. Why would I want her running around free?"

"I warned you that Buddy Corlew couldn't be trusted. He won't ever see the light of day again after this."

Jess held back the frosty retort she wanted to make as Black rushed away. When the elevator doors opened, Ricky Vernon exited. Black glared at him before boarding. Before Vernon could ask any questions, Harper ushered him into Henshaw's room. Jess spoke to Nicole Green, and then she called

Buddy to find out what in the world had happened. She felt reasonably confident he was not responsible for Amanda's escape. Not unless he had no other recourse. Whatever the case, *if* he was involved, he had better have one hell of a good explanation.

His line went straight to voicemail. "Dammit, Buddy. Where are you? Call me the instant you listen to this message."

Jess should call Lil and touch base with her surveillance detail.

Lori joined her in the corridor. "I spoke to your sister's surveillance detail. I've put them on alert regarding Brownfield's escape."

"Thanks. I was about to do that. I should call Lil and explain."

"I can hang out here while you step away if you'd like to have some privacy." Lori gestured to the end of the hall and the window there.

"I'll only be a minute," Jess promised.

"Take your time." Lori squeezed her arm.

Jess gave her a grateful nod and hurried along the carpeted floor. She stared out the window as her sister's phone rang. Lil had a family. She'd given up nursing to be a full time wife and mother. Motives and methods for murder never entered her mind. She didn't have to worry about obsessed serial killers and haunted reverends or the psychopathy of a possible half sister like Amanda Brownfield. At least she hadn't until Jess came back to town.

For days now, she'd hidden the ugly truth from her sister to protect her. What a joke. Lil was one of the strongest people Jess knew. What she'd really been covering up was her own inability to accept that she wasn't any closer to the truth than she'd been a week ago. She didn't have the answers. Not yet anyway. But that didn't give her the right to keep what she'd learned from the people she loved.

"It's about time you called," Lil said instead of hello. "You were supposed to call me on Monday and tell me how the Baron barbecue went. Was Nina there?"

"I'm sorry, Lil. Work got in the way." This was the same excuse she'd been using for twenty years. "Listen, that Brownfield woman I told you about has escaped custody. Your surveillance detail will be keeping an eye out for her."

"What about her little girl?"

"She's safe. Everyone's on the lookout for the mother. I want you to be extra careful. Her fixation with me could spill over to you."

The hesitation that lingered before Lil spoke again had Jess's heart pounding harder.

"I've decided to buy a gun, Jess. I'm at home alone so often it just feels necessary."

The announcement was certainly an unexpected one. Lil hated guns. "Let's start with signing you up for the proper weapons training first."

"I mean it, Jess. All this stuff with Spears is making me paranoid."

"I understand. We'll take care of it. I promise." Jess braced. "Lil, we need to talk." The warning that she had another call sounded in Jess's ear.

"I'm home," Lil reminded her with a sigh. "I'm always home. It's really empty with the kids gone. Why don't you come right now?"

"I have another call. I'll call you back. Stay safe." Jess ended the call and accepted the incoming one. "Harris."

"I told you Eric could get me out."

Jess stilled. "Amanda, I need to know where you are. Right now."

She laughed. "You always sound so serious and I keep telling you the same thing. There is nothing you can do to stop this, Jess. He's coming for you. Everything else is smoke and mirrors."

"Not you, Amanda. You're my sister remember? Sisters stick together no matter what. Tell me where you are and I'll come. Just me. No one else."

A beat of silence echoed.

"Why didn't you tell me about the dark-haired man who drives the Infiniti?" Jess asked when Amanda remained silent. "He brought you pictures of me."

"You'll know everything soon, Jess. Don't resist." Another hesitation. "It'll be better that way."

"Amanda, where are you. Let me help you."

"Come to the water, Jess. You know where. I'm leaving something there for you."

CHAPTER FIFTEEN

Standing on the Comer Bridge above the river where her parents had glimpsed their final view of daylight before slipping beneath the dark surface, Jess surveyed the water and the shoreline once more.

If Amanda had left something for her, she'd hidden it well.

Sheriff Foster and a dive team searched the water beneath the bridge. They'd found nothing so far. Jess had called Foster en route. By the time she and Lori arrived, the search was underway.

She told herself this was nothing more than another diversion Spears had set in motion. As much as she wanted to believe that, deep down inside, Jess sensed this time was different somehow.

"The divers found something," Lori said from her vantage point at the guardrail.

Jess started that way and her cell phone rang. Hoping it was Dan, she stopped to check the screen. *Gant.* "Dammit." He'd called twice already. She tossed her phone back into her bag. Black had evidently gone straight to Gant about her insubordination. She doubted her former boss would be surprised. He knew her too well, but that wouldn't prevent him from reminding her of all the reasons her behavior was unreasonable and unacceptable.

As Jess reached the guardrail, Lori placed a hand on her arm. "It's Amanda Brownfield."

At some point along this journey, Jess had thought she was prepared for almost anything. After all she'd seen in her career, what could possibly shake her?

This shook her…hard.

"Call Dr. Baron," she said, her voice not as strong as she'd prefer. "Tell her we need a preliminary on Amanda tonight. I'll work it out with Foster."

The words were scarcely out of her mouth when two black SUVs parked behind the other official vehicles on the side of the road at the entrance to the bridge. The doors flew open and Chief Black, as well as four agents, emerged.

Now the real battle began.

By the time Jess reached the shoreline, Black and Agent Todd Manning from the Birmingham FBI Field Office, were arguing with Sheriff Foster. Jess could hardly take her eyes from the ominous black body bag. Her last exchange with Amanda sifted through her thoughts. On some level, it was difficult to see Amanda as a victim but, in actuality, that was exactly what she was.

Black's firm tone, punctuated by Manning's furious one, drew Jess's attention. Foster wiped the sweat from his brow, settled his hat back in place, and bided his time while the others explained the legalities of why he would need to turn over the body ASAP.

Jess figured her best option was to let them hash it out. She was banking on the probability that the small town cop with the big hat and the cowboy boots was on her side.

"Well, gentlemen," Foster began, "I'm afraid you'll have to take your requests up with Sheriff Griggs down in Jefferson County. You see, I already turned all this over to him and his representative." Foster gestured to Jess. "Our coroner already pronounced the victim and Jeb Cardin over at the funeral home's sending a hearse to transport the body to the Jefferson County Coroner's office as we speak."

Jess didn't see any need to stay and listen as Black and Manning challenged Foster's declaration. She and Lori headed for her Mustang. The somber black hearse arrived as they pulled away, making Jess feel cold. Maddie's mother, whatever her issues and whatever she was guilty of, was dead. Now the little girl was an orphan in the truest sense of the word.

Jess knew that feeling.

Lori executed a U-turn and drove away from the place that somehow continued to provoke change in Jess's life.

She checked her cell to see if Dan or Buddy had returned her calls. No missed calls. Why couldn't she reach Dan? She'd given a message to his secretary in addition to the voicemails she'd left him. And where was Buddy? Frustrated, she left another voicemail for him with an update on Amanda.

"You don't think Buddy had anything to do with Amanda's escape, do you?"

Buddy was a lot of things, but stupid wasn't one of them. "When Amanda called she said something about Eric getting her out." Jess shook her head. "How do you spring someone out of the psych unit, for Christ's sake? She had a BPD guard in addition to the usual security measures."

"I put in a call to a friend of mine at the hospital."

"Did he have any information?" Black hadn't given Jess any of the details.

"He says a nurse took Amanda for an MRI. The nurse and the BPD uniform who accompanied her were found in the basement. Both had been shot and are in critical condition, but they're expected to make it."

"Were either of them able to give a statement?"

"He didn't know for sure."

Jess pressed her fingers to her temples and tried to ease the tension there. Buddy had promised to call her as soon as he spoke to Amanda. Dan should have called her back by now.

Where was everybody?

She stared at her phone and willed it to ring.

JEFFERSON COUNTY CORONER'S OFFICE,
8:30 P.M.

"I'm convinced you're trying to ruin my social life, Harris."

"I appreciate you staying late again."

Sylvia lifted a skeptical brow. "Don't make a habit of it." She looked Jess up and down. "Very nice." Her gaze lingered on the shoes. She sighed. "I don't know what Gina was thinking."

Jess was beginning to think that moments like this with Sylvia were about breaking the tension. Right now, as ready as Jess was to move on with this, she appreciated the break. "Comfort and practicality. You do recall those terms, don't you?"

"I deleted those from my vocabulary when I was twelve." Sylvia turned her attention back to the victim. "Let's get down to business, shall we?"

Jess surveyed Amanda's body. There was no question who had done this. Spears wanted Jess to know this was his work. The lacerations to her body, including her breasts, and the widespread bruising were all classic Player torture techniques. Her wrists and ankles bore ligature marks. The thigh and pelvic bruising along with vaginal tears was the sort of injuries Jess had seen repeatedly in his victims. Some of the damage was older, from her first meeting with Spears last Friday, Jess estimated, while others were fresh…only hours old.

The sutured lips were not typical Player handiwork. Was this some new point Spears wanted to make? The recent victims with the sutured lips appeared to all have one thing in common, they could have given Jess information. Spears had stopped them.

Speak no evil. Or, in this case, speak no truth.

"By the way," Sylvia noted, "Henshaw's tox screen was positive for Ketamine. The ME in Huntsville is sending me his preliminaries on Mooney and Skelton. I'm guessing he'll find the same."

"No surprise there." Ketamine was Spears drug of choice for his victims.

"She wasn't in the water very long," Sylvia announced, drawing Jess's attention back to the table and the woman who could be her half sister. "Skin isn't loose, wrinkling, or pimpled."

Amanda had called Jess shortly after noon. Foster's team had pulled her out of the water by five. Somewhere in between Spears or one of his sadistic followers had tortured and murdered her, and then had her dumped in the river.

Egotistical bastard.

"Let's check the mouth." Jess needed to know if there was another message. Any minute now Black or Manning could show up with a court order to take possession of the body. It would take a court order to override Griggs' authority.

With sterile pincers and surgical scissors, Sylvia started the removal process. Jess's cell sounded. She dug for it in her bag and checked the screen. *Dan.* Her heart leapt. Thank God. "I have to take this."

Peeling off a glove, Jess hurried from the room. Lori came out right behind her, had a look around, and then took a short walk down the corridor.

Jess swiped the screen and accepted Dan's call. "You okay?"

"I'm hanging in there." He sounded exhausted and disgusted. He had every right to be. This week had been hell on earth for him.

"I'm sorry about Meredith."

"Me, too." He sighed. "I heard about Amanda. How are you holding up?"

"It's strange." Jess shook her head. "I feel confused." How was she supposed to feel about this woman? She had no idea if she was her biological half sister and so what if she was. They hadn't formed a relationship. Amanda was a killer. The families of her victims would cheer when they heard the news about her death.

"I can imagine," Dan said. "When're you coming home?"

"I'm with Sylvia. She's doing a preliminary since I can't be sure Gant won't have Black or someone rush in and steal the body from me."

"Your standoff with Harold over at the Redmont is running rampant through the department grapevine." There was a hint of humor in his voice now.

"Gant pushed me into a corner. I had no choice."

Dan laughed softly. The sound made her wish she could go to him. "I love you, Jess. Come home as soon as you can. I need to hold you."

"Love you, too. Be there as soon as I can." Jess put her phone away. She could relax a little now that she'd heard from him.

Lori moved up beside her. "Everything okay?"

"As okay as it can be." Jess worried about Buddy. She hoped he wasn't at the bottom of that damned river, too. Gant was right. There was a new urgency in Spears latest moves. Anything could happen next.

"Can I ask you something, Jess?"

She pushed aside the disturbing thoughts. "You don't have to ask if you can ask. Of course you can." Had she been so distracted that she'd lost touch with her team? The whole week had felt disjointed and surreal.

"Did you want me at the Brownfield farm yesterday?"

Jess frowned. "Hayes said you'd headed over there with Cook to check out a hunch. I meant to ask you about it, but I've been a little distracted."

"I guess there was a lapse in communication. Hayes told me you wanted me over there with Cook. No problem, I was curious that's all." Her face told a different story. It was a problem and she was clearly frustrated.

Jess was more than a little frustrated herself. "If Hayes is—"

The door to the exam room opened. Sylvia poked her head out. "Spears left a message for you."

"We can talk about this later," Lori assured her.

Heart banging against her ribs, Jess followed Sylvia back to the autopsy table. A plastic Ziploc bag had been removed from Amanda's mouth. Inside was a wallet size photo. Jess pulled on new gloves and carefully removed the photo from the bag. The image of big brown eyes and a wide smile framed by long, dark hair stared out at her. Hand shaking, she turned the photo over.

And then there were four…only one to go until it's your turn, Jess. Can't wait.

The note was signed *Eric.*

Jess turned to Lori. "Get Gant on the line for me."

Only one to go…before it was *her* turn.

CHAPTER SIXTEEN

Buddy Corlew parked the Volkswagen Beetle he'd
borrowed from a friend, shut off the headlights and
waited. After what he'd seen on the news, he wasn't
so sure showing up for this little tete-a-tete was such
a good idea. His cell vibrated and he checked the
screen knowing full well it would be Jess.

He ignored her call the way he had all the others. She would only try talking him into coming in.
Not happening until he was done. If he was right,
he was too close to let anything or anyone get in his
way. In the end, if he survived, Jess would thank him.

If he were wrong, it wouldn't be the first time.
He just hoped it wouldn't be the last.

He checked the time again. Where the hell was
he?

Headlights bobbed through the cemetery gate.
His instincts went on point. After all this time, if this
guy decided to turn on him now, Buddy was going
to be pissed.

The car parked and the driver opened his door and climbed out. No interior light came on to give him away. Cops and PIs knew interior lights were good for one thing, illuminating a target. With no sirens echoing in the distance and no blue lights pulsing through the darkness, Buddy breathed easier.

Detective Kelvin Roark walked the short distance and climbed into the passenger side of Buddy's borrowed car.

"What the hell took you so long?" Buddy didn't like to wait. Never had. His no good old man used to say he was born a grownup. From the beginning, he knew what he wanted and he demanded to have it. Not that he'd ever gotten anything from that drunken bastard.

"There was a last minute conference call with the FBI."

"I couldn't know that," Buddy gripped, "because you went dark on me around noon. What the hell happened?" Maybe he should have taken at least one of Jess's calls. If he had, he might have known what was going on.

"You need to lay low, Corlew. Amanda Brownfield's body was pulled from the river over in Jackson County about five this evening."

The news hit like a sucker punch.

"Same MO as the others," Roark went on. "Lips were sewn shut. This time Spears put the photo of his latest victim in her mouth. Gant says he's escalating. Six is his number. He left a note on the back of the photo saying there was one more to go before it would be Harris's turn."

Buddy tightened his fingers around the steering wheel. "Was Brownfield tortured?"

"Oh yeah. Tortured and subjected to some rough ass sex."

Whatever Amanda Brownfield had been, no one deserved to die like that.

"I guess cutting her loose was a mistake." Roark laughed.

"I did not cut her loose." When Buddy had walked out of that hospital, he'd been alone. His last image of Brownfield was of her shackled to the damned bed.

"Everybody thinks you did," Roark warned with a little extra pleasure. "The uniform who was guarding her says he never saw the shooter. Nurse didn't either. No video in the basement to show what happened. Black intends to hang you for this one. If they catch you, I can't help you. You got that? This arrangement will be over. If I was you, I'd be getting the hell out of Dodge."

"Black's been trying to hang me since I was a rookie cop taking his orders," Buddy argued. Nothing new there. "And there's no need for you to be concerned about my expectations, Roark, I fully understand the boundaries of our arrangement."

"Good, because I have to tell you, Corlew, Black may just do it this time. The woman is dead. You were her last visitor. Maybe you wanted her dead and copied the MO of these latest murders to put the blame somewhere else. Or maybe you're one of Spears's followers."

Buddy leaned toward him. Roark flinched. "What the hell you doing here if you think I might be one of Spears's followers?"

"I never said I thought that." Roark laughed nervously. "I came here to warn you. This isn't going away. Black is out for blood. *Your* blood."

"What about Burnett? Any new evidence against him?"

Even in the darkness, Buddy could feel Roark scrutinizing him. "I'm beginning to think you're worried about Burnett."

"You going soft in the head, Roark? Burnett's been a pain in my ass since I was a sophomore in high school. It was never enough that he was rich, he had to knock me down at everything I attempted. Are you forgetting he fired me from the Force?" Buddy pounded the steering wheel with the heel of his hand to punctuate his words. "Screw it! Get outta my car, Roark. I don't need this crap from you."

"Okay, okay." Roark blew out a big breath. "This situation is getting dicey. Burnett retained Frank Teller. He's got his big shot investigative team crawling all over this. It's making me nervous. That's all."

Buddy was glad it was dark because he couldn't stop his lips from curling into a smile. "What can I do to help? The sooner we toss Burnett outta there, the better off the department will be."

"Damn straight," Roark agreed. "Black deserved that promotion four years ago. Pratt wanted young blood in the office. A new more progressive attitude for the city. I guess he learned the hard way that you can't own a guy like Burnett."

"Ain't that the truth?" Buddy commiserated. "You got screwed, too. You should've made captain a long time ago."

"It's coming," Roark assured him. "Burnett is going down."

"With Dority dead, you think there's enough evidence." Buddy shrugged. "I mean, Prescott's case isn't that strong. You need something else?"

Roark laughed. "I don't think so, man. Between the evidence in the Allen case and then this Dority thing, Burnett is finished."

Buddy needed Roark to be more specific. "We both know Burnett is no killer. How the hell did that evidence end up at his house?"

"Who cares? Just be grateful. Keep your head down, Corlew, until this Brownfield thing blows over," Roark advised. "I may still need you. You owe me."

Roark got out and swaggered back to his car. Those last words kept ringing in Buddy's ears. *You owe me.* Unfortunate, but true. Buddy shut off the recording device he'd hidden in his dash and drove away.

Tonight's meeting hadn't cleared Dan but it did point to a conspiracy. Would that be enough? With Amanda Brownfield's escape hanging over his head, Buddy wasn't sure how much longer he could prod Roark for information. For the good it had done so far. Roark claimed not to know who was planting the evidence against Burnett. Someone damned sure planted Allen's wedding band and cell phone.

Putting the cemetery behind him, Buddy headed to the address Rosey had under surveillance. Leaving that location had been a difficult choice but Roark had demanded a meeting. Buddy couldn't afford to make him suspicious.

Now if what he'd learned from Amanda Brownfield panned out, he might just come out of this barrel of shit smelling like a hero.

Damn. It sucked to think what she'd gone through before she died. When Buddy had first entered her room, she'd tried to play him. She'd wanted information on Jess. Buddy had sensed that the questions meant more to her on a personal level than Amanda wanted anyone to know.

A woman who had killed her own mother and the guy she was sleeping with wasn't to be trusted in any capacity, yet he'd picked up on her genuine desire to know more about Jess. Not just for Spears either.

Now she was dead.

Had she known Spears was going to kill her? Maybe that was the reason she'd given something to Buddy she hadn't given to anyone else. She'd asked him to lean closer and she'd stolen a kiss before he could react. Then she'd whispered a phrase and said she'd seen it on a license plate across the street from where she'd met with Spears that one time.

Maybe she was screwing with him. Buddy couldn't say. Whatever her goal, the information was worth consideration. He'd gotten a pal at the DMV to run the Alabama plate, *1PERCNT*.

The address was in a particularly prestigious neighborhood in Birmingham high atop Red Mountain. Buddy had a real estate friend who was looking into recent purchases in the area. For now, he intended to watch this location in case Amanda was telling the truth. If Spears was there, he'd have to come out sometime. Until then, another borrowed car would be Buddy's hotel room.

Twenty minutes later, Buddy parked right behind the BMW Rosey Cunningham had borrowed from his chiropractor. He and Buddy would exchange cars since a Beetle would stand out like an A cup in a wet T-shirt contest.

Buddy grabbed his bag, eased out of the Beetle, and moved to the driver's side of the BMW. Rosey had already slid over the console and into the passenger seat. Buddy tossed him the keys to the Beetle. "Any activity?"

"Lights came on upstairs about an hour ago. No departures and no arrivals. Driveway sensors are in place. So's the one on the car."

About five this evening a limo had arrived. Pulled into the garage and then departed about fifteen minutes later. The driver had dark hair and sunglasses had shielded his face. The heavy tint on the passenger compartment windows prevented a visual on the passenger. The irony that the limo arrived here about the same time Amanda's body was pulled from the river was not lost on Buddy.

He wanted to get this guy. Maybe more than he'd ever wanted anything.

"Good deal, Rosey." The sensors would notify Buddy through his cell if anyone passed on the street or entered the driveway of the property under surveillance. He didn't plan on sleeping but he was only human. His bag was loaded with power drinks and protein snacks. Everything else, weapons, binoculars, portable urinal, were right here in the Beemer.

"Call me when you need to go somewhere or sleep," Rosey said before heading out.

Buddy grunted. He had no intention of leaving until he had confirmation that Eric Spears was in that house.

Then, he was taking him down.

CHAPTER SEVENTEEN

With Dan at her side, Jess climbed the stairs slower than usual. They'd been on a ninety-minute conference call with Gant and a representative from the other agencies making up the Joint Task Force. The image of those divers pulling Amanda's pale body from the water along with the photo of the young woman Spears had taken and the pages from her mother's journal kept whirling through her head like debris in a tornado.

Four women were missing. As of last Friday, the first two were still alive according to Amanda. She had seen them in the torture room Spears had created somewhere in this city. Spears wasn't bold enough to show his face anywhere around Birmingham at this point. Every media outlet within a hundred mile radius reminded the public to be on the lookout for him in every newscast and in every newspaper released.

The trouble was, there was no way to warn the citizens about his followers. These people, like

Amanda and Richard Ellis, could come from any-where at any time.

Gant hadn't mentioned that Jess was off the case again. Hell, there was no separating her from the case.

She glanced up at the man beside her and wished she could take away the worry marring his face.

At least they were home now. The light at the top of the stairs beckoned to her. She needed to go inside with Dan and close out the world.

A low growled issued from the landing a few steps away. Dan held her back.

"Was that a dog?" Jess hoped these new shoes were as good at rushing down stairs as they were at climbing up them.

"I think so." Dan moved up a step.

A furry head peeked over the edge of the landing. Jess gasped. "It is a dog!"

"It's a puppy," Dan clarified. "Come here, boy."

The dog drew back as Dan ascended another step.

"What if it bites you?" Jess had never had a dog. She and Lil had once had a lazy old cat named Tom. He'd died when she was nine. Her mother had made a big production of giving him a proper burial in the backyard.

Jess moved cautiously up to join Dan on the landing. He was crouched down scratching the yel-low Lab behind the ears. She might never have had a dog, but she'd made it a point to learn the breeds. Encountering dogs was a hazard of every cop's life.

"He won't bite." Dan ruffled his hair. "He must be lost. No tags or collar."

"He might have one of those chips." Someone was no doubt missing a dog as cute as this one.

Dan stood. "If he's still here in the morning, I'll have a veterinarian friend of mine check him out."

"You think he needs food or water?" Jess unlocked the door, leaned inside, and entered the security code so the system would stop its infernal beeping.

"I'll take care of him. You need a long hot soak."

She liked how he was always thinking of her. "That's one order I'm happy to take."

As soon as the hot water was running, she stripped off her clothes. She studied her body in the full-length mirror that hung on the bathroom door. She didn't look pregnant yet. Too soon, she supposed, but she had gained some weight. Her next shopping spree would be with Lil. Her sister couldn't wait to help with the maternity clothes and with decorating a nursery. The nursery would have to wait until she and Dan had a house.

Tomorrow, she had to find time to spend with Lil. There was a lot they had to talk about. She'd hoped to find that time today but she'd ended up having to call her sister and reschedule. Lil had made a list of the shops and websites they were going to visit. Jess smoothed a hand over her tummy. She was so glad she could share this experience with her sister.

Grateful to have this day behind her, she climbed into the tub and sank into the warm water.

Now this, she moaned, felt good. Closing her eyes, she relaxed and let the water work its magic on her tense muscles. She blocked the sounds and images from the day and concentrated on Maddie swinging and laughing. How could a child who had probably witnessed inconceivable atrocities be so happy?

Jess squeezed her eyes tighter. She didn't want to think about this anymore.

As hard as she tried, she couldn't stop the questions. Damn Buddy Corlew. He should have called her back by now. What had he gotten himself into? The hospital security footage showed Buddy coming out of Amanda's room, and then ten minutes later a nurse arrived to take her for an MRI. The MRI never happened. The final image of Amanda on any hospital security camera showed her alone and headed through the parking garage, dressed in the nurse's scrubs, the sling and restraints gone.

She'd walked away smoking a cigarette.

If Spears had her picked up and brought to him, it had to have happened fast. Gant and Black had every realtor in the city on alert. What houses had been sold, rented, or leased in the past ninety days? What houses were sitting vacant with no activity? From Amanda's description of the house, it was in one of the city's more affluent neighborhoods.

"He could be right next door." Jess shuddered at the thought.

Dan rapped on the door before easing it open. "How about a glass of juice? It's grape?"

"Wine does come from grapes," she agreed. Might as well look at the bright side. There would be no wine for her for a long time to come. They had tried the non-alcohol variety and it was bad.

He sat down on the floor next to the tub and offered her the wine glass with the grape juice. "Presentation is everything."

Jess laughed. "Absolutely." She sipped her juice, savored the warmth of the water and the opportunity to stare at the man she loved. He'd shed his jacket and tie, and shoes, she noticed. She cradled her glass. "I'm really worried about Buddy. I'm the reason he went to see Amanda. After we met with Wanda, he wanted a stab at getting information from her."

"If," Dan qualified, "he helped her escape, that was his decision. Not yours."

"He wouldn't do that." Jess shook her head. "When Amanda called, she led me to believe it was Spears."

Dan propped an elbow against the rim of the tub and braced his head in his hand. "Buddy makes some shady moves under the umbrella of being a PI. He doesn't always follow the rules and often not the law." He scoffed. "What am I saying? He never follows the rules. He may have taken a calculated risk—exchanged help for information."

"If that were true," Jess countered, "I'd have the information by now. He was talking to her for me."

"I'm just saying we don't know what they said to each other in that hospital room."

"I guess we'll know when Buddy can tell us." *If he wasn't dead.* The thought scared Jess. Dammit, she didn't want him to be dead. She didn't want any of this. What she did want was the truth—the truth about her parents and the truth about the Brownfields. She'd had no time to look at the pages from her mother's journal or Henshaw's notes.

Tomorrow, she was going to hunt McPherson down and make him talk. He had known her father. Strangers weren't invited to intimate family barbecues. She had the picture to prove it.

"This morning I drove by some of the houses Mom suggested."

"Did you see any you liked?" They had to find time to house hunt.

"Some. Mostly, it was something to do to take my mind off *things.*"

Jess sat up, water splashing, and set her glass on the tile floor. She reached up and caressed his jaw. "I can't imagine how hard all this must be."

He threaded his fingers through her hair and kissed her with such desperation that fear slid through her. When he drew back, she searched his face. "Did something else happen?"

"I went to see Meredith this morning."

That lingering worry about Buddy vanished as panic spread through her. "*This* morning?"

Dan nodded. "She wouldn't talk to me. She kept saying she was sorry and trying to close the door in my face."

"I finally gave up and left. That's when I drove around and looked at the houses. I got to the office around eleven and Black was waiting to tell me about her murder." The pain on his face, in his words, was palpable.

"You did what you thought you had to do." Jess could certainly identify with the need to make things right.

"I don't understand why she made those allegations against me unless it was Pratt. And I sure as hell don't understand why anyone wanted to kill her."

"Where was her mother during all this?"

"In the bed right down the hall. She recognized my voice. After I left, the killer came in almost immediately. The exchange between Meredith and her killer was too quiet for her mother to recognize the person speaking or to hear the words that were said. The only thing her mother identified in her statement was my voice."

Jess searched his face. "Surely, she doesn't believe it was you."

"She's confused and devastated." He kissed the palm of her hand. "I want to point a finger at Pratt, but my head tells me he isn't capable of murder."

"We're all capable of murder given the right motivation." Jess contemplated what she knew about the mayor. "If it was Pratt, the question is did he plan it or was it an impulse? I would go with an impulse. He's a planner and a strategist, that's true, but plotting murder comes from a different place in ones psyche. The detectives investigating the case should pay close attention to the act itself. Was it sudden, sloppy, and drawn out or was it quick and efficient? Those clues will point to the killer's frame of mind at the time."

"Enough talk about murder." Dan pulled the plug on the tub and reached for a towel. "I have other plans for you, the future Mrs. Burnett."

Jess stood, her legs wobbly from the soak and the desire now coursing through her.

Dan slowly caressed her body with the fluffy towel, and then he wrapped it around her. "We need to decide on a ring," he reminded her. "People will start to talk if we don't get a ring on that finger soon."

He scooped her up and she wrapped her arms around her neck. "I will love whatever ring you choose."

"Are you sure about that?" He pressed his forehead to hers. "Few women would put a choice like that in a man's hands."

"I trust you completely." Right now, she wanted him *completely.*

Dan carried her from the steamy room. The cooler air made her shiver.

He grinned. "Don't worry, I'll chase those chills away in about thirty seconds."

Jess frowned. "What's that sound?" Scratching at the door, she decided.

"The puppy," they said together.

"Did you feed him?"

"A piece of ham and a slice of bread."

Jess chewed her lip. "What about water?"

"I put a bowl out there when I fed him."

"You think he's okay?"

"He'll be fine."

Dan laid her gently on the bed. Jess smiled as he stripped off his shirt. She loved watching him undress. His muscular body was more beautiful to her now than when he'd been a teenager.

He reached for his fly.

The puppy yelped.

Jess sat up, holding the towel to her chest. "He sounds like he's hurt."

"He's not hurt."

"We should check on him." Jess got off the bed and started for the door.

Dan got there first. "I'll check on him."

He checked the monitors to ensure no one was on the landing or the stairs before disarming the security system, unlocking, and opening the door. The puppy shot through the door before Dan could stop him. He rushed straight up to Jess and started licking her legs.

She didn't really like dogs, she reminded herself as she crouched to pet him. "You're so clean and cute. You must be someone's pet."

"Come on, boy," Dan urged. "You're interfering with my plans."

The puppy looked at Dan but immediately turned his attention back to Jess. "Maybe I can lure him back to the door." She could at least try.

"I don't think so," Dan said with a pointed look at her towel-clad body.

"Oh." Jess winced. "Guess not."

With the promise of another slice of bread, the puppy followed Dan onto the landing. Dan locked up and rearmed the security system while Jess climbed back onto the bed and waited for him.

He headed in that same direction. "I think I was about to do this." He reached for his zipper.

The yelping and scratching started again with renewed purpose.

Dan's face fell. Jess laughed. "I think we're going to have to let him inside."

With a sigh, Dan went back through the steps and opened the door. Jess enjoyed the show as he attempted to calm the puppy and cajole him onto a blanket by the door. Jess had a feeling that wasn't going to happen.

Eventually, the dog was in the bed with them. She remembered giggling at Dan one last time before sleep stole her away.

CHAPTER EIGHTEEN

"We're crawling all over this city," Chief Black assured Agent Gant. "Any additional manpower the Bureau can spare would be greatly appreciated."

Another teleconference this morning had eaten up an entire hour already. Jess was anxious to get back to her office and start analyzing the notes and journal pages the reverend had left. Whatever Henshaw had discovered in her mother's diary, it appeared to have cost him his life. Why hold onto it all these years? Had the Spears situation prompted the reverend to act on old concerns? Was that why he'd suddenly dug up the diary and started following Jess in the news?

"Sheriff Griggs has his deputies working over-time to support the search for Spears," Dan chimed in, drawing Jess back to the briefing.

"We also have quite a number of civilian volunteers on standby," Black added.

"We won't go there unless we have no other choice," Dan warned. "The last thing we need is a

216

hothead getting trigger happy. We'll stick with professionally trained police personnel for now."

Black turned his hands up. "I believe our choices are growing more limited every day. How many more people will die before we stop him?"

"Chief Burnett is right," Gant announced, silencing all in the room. "Calls to action have already gone out in the media. Having the community's eyes on the lookout is a far more valuable tool than risking an encounter with Spears during the course of a grid search."

"Spears knows how to hide," Jess reminded the members of the Task Force. "He's been hiding for years without being caught. The average citizen armed with outrage and a weapon won't find him. He would use a move like that against us. Manipulating people is one of his strongest assets. We don't need to give him anyone else to use in his twisted game."

Black nodded in what appeared to be agreement, but he didn't meet Jess's gaze. Challenging his suggestion wasn't her intent. She knew Spears, understood his motives, Black needed to grasp the concept that her goal was not to usurp his authority. It was to stop Spears.

Spears was nearing the end of his game, his focus was narrowing. Gant had confirmed that all chatter on the Internet between Spears and his followers had stopped or was buried so deep it would take years and teams of cyber forensic analysts to ferret it out. He was eliminating risk. The fewer people who knew details about the final stages of his plan, the better. This was the first time, to her knowledge, he had worked with such a large cast of characters. But then, reaching her wasn't as easy as plucking the innocent from their unsuspecting daily lives. To reach her, he had to depend on others to provide distraction. Jess hoped that need would be his downfall.

The rustling of fabric and the scooting of chairs signaled the briefing had concluded. Jess stood and gathered her notes and bag.

Dan delayed her departure as Black, Roark, Manning, and the other agent drifted out the door, too caught up in their own conversation to care that she and Dan stayed behind.

"I promise to be careful," she said before he could remind her.

"Good." He squeezed her hand. "We just have to get through this. *Safely.*"

Jess understood all too well. Spears wasn't their only issue. Black had told Dan they needed to meet privately after the briefing. That volatile mix of anger and pain she'd been suffering so much lately, roiled inside her now. She didn't care that they were in the department conference room and anyone could walk in, she went on tiptoe and kissed him on the cheek. "We will get through this." She draped her bag onto her shoulder. "I have to go. The team's waiting for me."

Dan gave her a nod before making his own preparations to leave. Jess hesitated at the door to look back at him one last time. *Please let this be over soon.*

Hayes waited for her in the corridor.

"How long before Cook's exam results are available?" she asked the lieutenant.

"Ten to fourteen days."

Cook met the necessary age, education, and experience requirements. As long as he passed the written test, Jess felt confident she could make the promotion happen.

"I appreciate you helping him prep for the exam."

"Just trying to do my part as a member of the team."

Jess hoped that was the case. "Remember that, Hayes." She hesitated, forcing him to stop as well. "I need you to understand that I will not tolerate manipulation or deception." She opted not to mention Lori's complaint specifically. "You may have crossed those lines in the past, but know this, if you cross one again, it will be the last time you do so as a member of my team."

"Got it."

"I hope so, Lieutenant. I really do."

Back at the office, the rest of her team was hard at work. Jess scanned the case board. The timeline and all relevant photos and notes were in place.

"I'm impressed." That was fast work even for a team as good as this one.

Harper gestured to the photos of the reverend's room at the Redmont. "Henshaw had been keeping a timeline related to your activities since your abduction by Lopez."

Lori passed Jess a white binder at least three inches thick. "I pressured the folks at the lab into giving me a photocopy of all the pages we believe came from your mother's journal. I've arranged them in chronological order. There are pages missing or days she'd didn't journal like the week of the accident. Most are about you and your sister. The occasional one is about your father."

Jess couldn't speak for a moment. She hugged the binder to her chest. "Thank you. I'll share this with Lil."

Lori smiled. "No problem."

Jess left her bag and the binder on her desk. "Detective Wells, I'd like you to keep trying to reach Corlew. I haven't heard from him in more than twenty-four hours. If he's still out of touch, reach out to McPherson and see if he's heard from Corlew again." Jess turned to the case board, zeroed in on the retired ABI agent's photo. "In fact, see if Mr. McPherson would mind coming down to have a look at what we found at the hotel. I'd like his take on this."

"On it." Lori reached for the phone.

None of Henshaw's notes made any sense. They appeared more like the ramblings of a man who had drifted into dementia. Yet his neighbors and friends insisted the reverend was in good health and of sound mind.

What are you missing, Jess?

"I think there might be a pattern to his notes." Harper tapped one of the pages on the case board.

"Show me, Sergeant." Jess moved closer to the board and adjusted her glasses.

"Going in chronological order," Harper directed her attention to what they had deemed as page one, "if you take the first word in the first paragraph, then the second in the second paragraph and so on, this is what you have: *She came to me with an unbelievable story.*"

Pulse reacting to a spike in adrenaline, Jess resisted the urge to get carried away. "Could be coincidence."

"Look at this one." Hayes tapped the sixth page. "*He is trapped with death all around him.*"

Jess ordered herself to breathe. "So he's telling us that whoever came to him, presumably my mother, was terrified and had a story not quite believable." Sounded remarkably like the story Wanda had told Jess. "We need more than that, preacher," she muttered.

"Then the pattern changes," Harper said. "Unless you need me elsewhere, I'd like to stay on this."

"What if these are nothing more than the ramblings of an elderly man lapsing into dementia?" Jess worried they were chasing ghosts instead of leads?

"Harper's on to something," Hayes countered. He pointed to another page. "*The key protects the truth.*"

Jess read over the seemingly nonsensical words on the page, spotting the pattern. Then she moved to the photo of the key found in the reverend's mouth. "We need to find the music box or whatever that key opens."

Lori joined them at the case board. "McPherson is willing to look at what we have but he won't come here. I have photos of everything. I can go to him."

McPherson had no intention of making this easy. "Go," Jess relented. "You, too, Lieutenant. Maybe some of this will mean something to McPherson. Push him," she said to Lori. "He knows more than he's telling. While you're there, drop by the Brownfield farm and take another look for anything that key might open."

Hayes didn't look happy about the road trip. What was it about this guy that made him intent on challenging her orders?

"Manning's not going to give us any trouble?" Lori asked.

"Gant caved after Sheriff Griggs got involved." Jess couldn't adequately express how pleased she was that he'd backed her up. "We have access to any and all aspects of this investigation."

"Bout time." Lori grabbed her bag and keys. "I'm driving," she said to Hayes.

He shrugged. "Fine by me."

"Sergeant, carry on with your decoding."

Jess walked over to Cook's desk. He was still hunkered over his laptop. "Any luck?" She dragged Lori's chair over next to his.

"No postings for lost dogs matching that description on craigslist or AL.com." He glanced over at Harper whose back was turned to them. "I posted the pic you sent me in the lost and found. Hopefully, if someone's out there looking for him, they'll respond." He made a face. "You have to be careful though. Someone might try to claim him just so they can do bad things like use him in dog fights or sell him for testing or something." Cook considered the photo of the dog. "Looks like a thoroughbred. He could be valuable to a breeder. Anyone could try and claim him."

"I'll need some sort of proof of ownership." Jess nodded. "Thanks for the pointer. You have a dog?"

Cook grinned. "Two. A Lab and a Golden Retriever. They keep me company."

"I really appreciate it. Someone is probably franticly searching for him." He really was cute, as puppies went.

"I'll call some of the vets around town and Animal Services to see if a yellow Lab pup has been reported missing. Don't worry, Chief, I'll field any calls on my cell."

"Thanks." Jess rolled Lori's chair back to her desk.

"Chief?"

Jess turned back to the officer she hoped would be a detective before the year was out.

"Thanks for the recommendation. Detective Wells told me she'd never seen such an outstanding one."

"You earned it, Chad." Jess had gotten word this morning that Cook's package was missing her written recommendation since she hadn't known in advance he was taking the exam. She and Lori had put it together first thing. Since, technically, she had been the one to suggest Cook start prepping for the exam, she decided not to ask him why he hadn't discussed moving forward with her. "You're a great asset to this team."

His cheeks reddened the slightest bit. Had she ever been that young?

The door opened and a man poked his head in and looked around, his gaze landing on Jess. Harper was blocking his path before he stepped across the threshold.

"You lost, sir?"

"I'm here to see Chief Harris."

Jess studied the man. Tall. Medium build. Middle-aged, salt and pepper hair. Distinguished. He looked vaguely familiar. "I'm Chief Harris."

"Robert Ellis." The man's expression seemed to harden right before her eyes. "I'm here to find out what happened to my brother."

Surprised, Jess directed him to her desk. "Have a seat, Mr. Ellis."

Harper returned to his work at the case board but kept an eye on Ellis.

Ellis stood before her desk until Jess had taken her seat.

"I'm very sorry about your brother, Mr. Ellis."

"Bob. Call me Bob, please."

"Bob." She indicated the chair next to him.

"I've been out of the country for three months," Bob explained as he took a seat. "I only returned two days ago. I was stunned to learn Richard was dead. The Boston police told me nothing. So I came here."

Jess couldn't decide if Bob was distraught over his brother's death or angry. The biggest question at the moment, however, was how had they missed a brother? "Excuse my confusion but I was under the impression Richard didn't have any family."

Bob dropped his head for a moment. "My brother and I have been estranged for years. I can't even remember the last time we spoke or saw each other." He let go a heavy breath. "I want to understand what happened. He was accused of murder? Then he killed himself in his holding cell?"

Jess was tempted to ask him if he really wanted to hear this. Then she thought of Amanda Brownfield and the uncertainty surrounding her own father. "We believe Richard committed a number of murders, some in this country and some in others. I can only speculate about the older murders, but here, in Birmingham, he was a co-conspirator in at least four. He may have committed suicide to avoid a trial and years on death row."

Bob was silent for a time. "All these years." He laughed softly, agonizingly. "I assumed that one day we'd put the past behind us and resume a relationship. That won't happen now."

"I wish I could tell you more." This was the part Jess disliked the most about her job. What did you say to the family? Your brother was a sociopath who liked ripping people's hearts out? Maybe not.

"Where is he?"

In hell, Jess imagined. "Since we weren't aware of any next of kin and this was his current city of residence, his body would have been turned over to a local funeral home for burial." Jess leaned to one side. "Officer Cook, would you help Mr. Ellis—Bob," Jess smiled at the man, "locate the funeral home that took care of Richard Ellis?"

"Yes, ma'am." Cook reached for the phone.

Jess stood. "I'm so sorry for your loss, Bob. If you'll have a seat over there with Officer Cook, he'll make sure you find your brother."

Ellis pushed to his feet. "Thank you for being so kind in spite of what he did. I don't know what made him become such a devil."

Jess accepted the hand he extended. "Safe travels back to Boston, Bob."

Before she could turn her attention back to the case board, her cell rang. She unearthed it from her bag. *Sylvia.* Tension gripped her. "You have something new on Amanda?"

"I have the DNA results."

Jess held her breath.

"You and Amanda shared a parent, Jess."

For several seconds Jess couldn't grasp the words she needed to say. "Thank you for taking care of this for me. Any word on…the other?"

"I should have the results on the fetus in the next forty-eight hours."

Jess thanked her again and ended the call. She couldn't share this with anyone else right now. Not until she talked to Dan and to Lil. She grabbed her bag and walked over to Harper. "Sergeant, I have to see my sister. Call Nicole Green and ask her if we can have a few minutes with Maddie. I'll have Lil meet us there."

How did she explain this to Lily when she didn't understand any of it herself?

MOTT STREET RESIDENCE, NOON

"She's beautiful." Lil swiped at her eyes with the back of her hand.

"She is."

"When will they tell her about her mother?"

"Soon, I suppose."

Lil crossed her arms over her chest. "I can't believe he did this."

Her sister was angry now. The shock and sadness would come later. "I will find out why." Somehow. With Amanda and her mother dead, it might not be easy.

"You've known this for a week and you didn't tell me?"

"I've only known for a few days." Jess put her arm around her sister's shoulder and watched Maddie romp around the backyard for a few moments. "Until about two hours ago, all I had was a murderer's story, Lil. I had to be sure before I put you through this emotional wringer. Trust me, it wasn't anyplace you wanted to be."

Lil sighed. "I know." She scrubbed her eyes again. "Our lives always seemed so normal. How could our father have been this kind of monster?"

That was the big question. "You don't remember any arguments or strange events?" Lil was only twelve when they died but a twelve year old should remember more than a ten year old.

Lil shook her head. "I remember going to the grocery store, getting ready for school, and family dinners. I remember all sorts of things, but no arguments or tension." She turned to Jess. "How could we not have felt the tension? When the kids were little, if Blake and I argued, they were always upset about it. How could we have been completely oblivious to something like this?"

"I wish I knew the answer." Jess had wracked her brain for memories and nothing suggesting trouble between her parents surfaced.

Lil frowned at Jess. "You didn't tell me Reverend Henshaw was murdered either. God. I read in the paper that he'd died, but not that he'd been so gruesomely murdered."

"He never visited you? You never ran into him at the grocery store? At a funeral or a wedding?"

Lil shook her head. "I haven't seen him since we were kids."

"He left me a key. I think maybe it goes to a music box. Didn't Mom have a jewelry box or something that played music?"

Lil mulled over the question. "Yes. Yes she did. It played…" She made a face. "I can't remember the name of the tune."

"Do you have any idea what happened to it?"

"Most everything was put in storage and God only knows what happened to it. Wanda probably stopped paying the rent and it ended up being sold."

"There was a storage unit?"

"Yeah. I think so. Wanda took me there once to pick up a box of clothes."

Why hadn't Wanda told her about this? "Did she ever mention it again?"

Lil shrugged. "You know we rarely saw her after Mom and Dad died. I've seen her a few times since the kids were born, but only in passing until recently."

"I remember she would show up from time to time and demand to take us with her." Jess had spent most of her life trying to forget those events. Maybe that was the reason she couldn't recall any trouble between her parents.

"She was always drunk or high. Our foster parent would call the police." Lil sighed. "It's a miracle we survived and turned out to be normal."

"No kidding." Jess wasn't so sure about the normal part or the miracle, but she could definitely use one right now.

Actually, she would settle for some straight answers.

CHAPTER NINETEEN

Dan finished the last of the documents that required his signature then tossed the folder into the outbox. On second thought, he grabbed the folder and carried it to his secretary.

"I believe that clears my desk."

Shelia nodded, her face cluttered with emotion. "Chief Black called. He's on his way up."

Dan gave her a nod. "When he arrives, send him on in."

Frank Teller had called Dan already. Pratt had signed the papers. As of close of business today, Dan was officially on administrative leave until the Allen and Dority cases were resolved. No surprise. No need for Teller or the union rep to be here for the official proclamation.

Dan returned to his desk without bothering to close the door. Black would explain how this would play out. He had a duty to carry out, nothing personal.

If Jess were here, she would argue that point.

A rap on his door had Dan bracing. When he'd accepted this position four years ago, he certainly hadn't expected things to end this way.

"Chief," Harold Black acknowledged as he strode across the room.

"Harold." Dan hadn't intended to sound bitter, but somehow he did.

Harold stopped in front of his desk and passed a thin manila folder to Dan. "You know as well as I do this is only temporary. As soon as we have this mess with Allen and Dority straightened out, you'll be back. Consider it a vacation. You'll have time to find a new home and buy a new car. I'm sure you have plenty to keep you busy for a couple of weeks."

"I do." Dan tossed the folder on his desk without looking at it. It wasn't necessary.

"I'll do my very best to uphold the standards you have set for this office, Dan, until your return."

"I'm confident you will. Roark will be acting over your division, I presume?"

"He will. Yes. Did you have a different candidate in mind?"

Dan shook his head. "Roark is the obvious choice."

"He's a good man."

"I'll have my desk cleared by the end of the day."

Harold gave another nod and then he left.

A hesitant rap at his door drew Dan's attention there once more. *Tara.*

"Chief, I picked up those boxes." She placed the boxes between the chairs in front of his desk. "Is there any way I can help?"

"I've got it, Tara. Thank you."

She dabbed at her eyes. "Yes, sir."

At the door, she hesitated, looked back once more. "Shelia and I know you'll be back, Chief. We're already planning a big celebration."

Dan gave her a smile but words escaped him.

For the next hour, Dan tucked all his personal possessions into the boxes. Instead of focusing on the task, he thought of all the things he needed to take care of. Harold hadn't been wrong about him needing time. The house and car were only the beginning.

As he closed the final box, he made another decision. He wasn't putting off what he wanted for another day. In fact, he intended to leave early and take care of at least one item on his to-do list today.

Since the announcement wouldn't hit the news until the five o'clock airing, he had time to talk to his parents as well. They deserved to hear this from him.

First, he had to tell Jess.

He picked up his cell and put through the call. The sound of her voice made him smile. "Hey."

"Hey yourself."

"I'm officially on administrative leave as of close of business today."

"I hope Black doesn't get too comfortable."

Dan had to smile at the fire in her tone. "I think he knows better."

"A wise man told me something recently that I've been holding onto."

"What's that?"

"We just have to get through this. *Safely.*"

His smile widened. "We will," he promised.

Before letting her go, he got an update on where she was. He'd feel a lot better when this day was over and she was at home with him.

Dan walked over to the window and looked out over the city he loved. He'd been wrong all those years ago when he'd left Jess in Boston. They would probably be celebrating their eighteenth or nineteenth anniversary and have a couple of kids running around by now if he hadn't walked away.

Instead, he'd spent the past twenty years building this career and discovering that no other woman could replace Jess. He banished those painful thoughts. They were together now and that was what mattered. He would spend however many years he had left being the very best husband and father he knew how.

On his desk, his cell vibrated with an incoming text. He checked the screen. *Private number.*

As he read the message, fury tightened his gut.

This is only the beginning of your end. Brace yourself, ex-Chief of Police Burnett.

"Son of a—"

The damned thing rang and he had to fight the impulse to throw it across the room. *Sylvia.* Jess had already told him about Amanda Brownfield's DNA results. Was there something new?

"Sylvia, I'm glad you called. I wanted to thank you—"

"Oh my God, Dan…"

Her voice shook so he barely made out her words. "Sylvia, what's wrong?"

"It's Nina. She's missing."

"What?" She was in a private facility with top-notch security.

"We can't find her, Dan! She's gone."

"I'll be right there."

Dan rushed from his office. "I'll finish clearing out later today. Call Chief Black if anything comes up."

Nina Baron spent most of her time in a near catatonic state. She hadn't been outside a protected, structured environment in more than ten years.

How the hell could this have happened?

CHAPTER TWENTY

Jess waited, trying not to tap her foot with impatience, while Wanda settled into her chair with her tea.

"You said before," she began, unable to wait any longer, "there was a break in at the Irondale house after my parents died. What happened to the rest of their things? Photo albums? Furniture? Clothes? Things a burglar wouldn't be interested in." So far Lori hadn't been able to locate a police report on the alleged break in, but thirty two years was a long time and misdemeanor reports weren't always kept that long.

Wanda stirred creamer into her tea. "I...I have to think back."

On the drive here, Jess had formulated a theory she hoped was way off the mark.

"There wasn't a whole lot to speak of—not that was worth anything," Wanda commented.

Jess didn't remember seeing her mother wear jewelry beyond her wedding band so there might

235

not have been any jewelry. Little or no electronics of value, she suspected. Nothing she could think of that carried any real appeal for a burglar and that was the sticking point with Wanda's explanation. What was the intruder looking for?

"Where did their belongings go?"

"You know." Wanda set her tea aside. "I think there was a storage unit for a brief while."

You think? "Did you ever visit this storage unit?"

Wanda lifted her gaze to Jess, uncertainty showed there. "Yes."

"What did you do when you visited the unit?"

Wanda dropped her head. "I took things...to sell."

Outrage fired through Jess, but she held it back. "What kind of things?"

"First it was small things, like her tea service. Then the stereo and your father's golf clubs."

"So, piece by piece you sold everything? Is that what you're telling me?"

"There were some pieces of furniture, clothes, and pictures left but I couldn't keep up the rent payments so they were auctioned. I tried to get those things back but it was too late by the time I got the letter in the mail."

"Did you file a police report about the burglary at the house?"

She shook her head. "After they dismissed me when I made that other report I didn't see the point in bothering."

Wanda claimed Jess's mother warned her that if anything happened to them to have the police look into it. Wanda had filed the report, that much was true.

"Was there a music box or any other box that required a key for opening?" Jess asked, moving on.

Wanda's face lit up as if she'd remembered something important. "Helen did have a music box. She played it all the time for you girls." Wanda started to hum that haunting tune that wouldn't stay out of Jess's head.

"What happened to the music box?"

Wanda frowned. "It wasn't in the house. Either your mother did something with it or it was stolen. I never saw it after she died."

If the key wasn't to the music box, then to what? And how did Spears or the reverend end up with it?

The sound of her cell phone prevented Jess from asking her next question. *Lori* calling. "Excuse me a moment."

As she moved toward the kitchen, Jess appreciated the deep sound of Harper's voice as he chatted with Wanda to distract her.

"Is McPherson talking?" Jess certainly hoped so. At this point, he was the last known link to the Brownfields and all those murders. The families whose loved ones were buried on that farm deserved closure.

"He's dead," Lori said. "Same MO as the others, lips sutured closed. Sheriff Foster's on his way over here."

Damn. Jess shook her head. "All right. Have Foster call his coroner. We'll need him. I'm on my way."

Jess refused to allow the defeat nipping at her to take hold. Both McPherson and Amanda were dead. Now Spears could tell his version of the story. Creating his own account of the past was easy enough if he silenced everyone who knew the real story.

The stage was set with no unnecessary characters to get in the way of the outcome he desired.

Spears wanted it just between the two of them.

TUPELO PIKE, SCOTTSBORO, 4:15 P.M.

Official vehicles already lined the street outside McPherson's home when Jess arrived.

Harper parked his SUV. "Looks like the gang's all here."

"Let's hope McPherson gives us more dead than he did alive." Jess removed her sunglasses and tucked them into her bag.

"After working this area for over thirty years, the idea that he didn't know anything about the Brownfields is a little hard to swallow."

"So true, Sergeant." Jess emerged from the SUV and started for the house. She flashed her badge to the deputy protecting the perimeter.

Lori met them at the steps to the house. "The vic hadn't been dead more than half an hour when we arrived."

"Has anyone talked to the neighbors?"

"Hayes is canvasing the neighbors now. I stayed with McPherson."

"Is the coroner here?" Loren Adams, as Jess recalled.

"He's in the house."

"Good." Jess hesitated again. "What about Roger?"

Lori inclined her head toward the house. "He's in the backyard. Foster called a friend who takes in homeless animals. He's coming to pick him up."

Jess was glad the dog hadn't ended up a victim as well. "I'd say it's safe to speculate that the killer didn't venture into the backyard."

"I know I wouldn't have. How do you think that happened?" Lori asked. "The dog outside, I mean."

At the door, they donned protective shoe covers and gloves. "McPherson must have suspected trouble and put the dog out back to protect him."

"Doesn't that defeat the purpose?" Harper shrugged. "What's the point of a guard dog if he can't protect you?"

Lori rolled her eyes. "Can you tell he didn't have a dog growing up?"

"Who said I didn't have a dog growing up?" Harper contended as they joined the ongoing activities inside. Two of Foster's deputies waited on either side of the door inside the house. Both gave Jess a nod of acknowledgement.

McPherson sat in a recliner, a Beretta nine millimeter in one hand. Glued there, if the MO from the previous scenes carried through. Harper checked the weapon as best he could with it clutched in the victim's hand.

"Has his weapon been fired?" To Jess's way of thinking, an experienced lawman like McPherson would use his weapon to protect himself.

Harper shook his head. "Fully loaded with a round in the chamber."

Didn't make sense to Jess.

"I'm thinking he was drugged," Lori said. "Foster checked with the Liberty, a restaurant McPherson frequented, and he was there for lunch. He left the Liberty about one and we found him here at one forty-five. Foster is interviewing the restaurant employees. There was an open bottle of Mountain Dew in his truck. We're sending it to the lab as well."

"I doubt one of Spears's followers would have been able to ambush him otherwise," Jess agreed.

Blood had pooled on the floor around McPherson's chair from the slash to his throat. His T-shirt and jeans were soaked in crimson. Blood spatter had showered on the rug in front of his easy chair.

An evidence tech, on the opposite side of the room, was busy dusting various surfaces for prints. Adams, the Jackson County coroner, joined them in the living room and gave Jess a nod. "Since your detectives insisted I wait until you arrive, I assume I can begin now?"

"Yes. Thank you for your patience."

Adams gathered the tools he would need and leaned over the body. He clipped the knots then carefully removed the sutures. McPherson's mouth opened easily. Inside was the expected plastic baggie. He removed it and passed it to Jess. "There you go, Chief."

The note ignited the outrage she'd been trying to keep under control for days.

Poor Jess. Now you'll never know the truth unless you hear it from me. Eric

Jess passed the note to Harper to document and log into evidence. She walked to the kitchen and stared out the window over the sink. Poor Roger. The big German shepherd trotted the perimeter before stopping to claw at something in the middle of the yard, and then he ran to the back door in hopes of his master letting him in.

Who had McPherson been protecting by keeping quiet? She turned around and surveyed the kitchen. Buddy had searched this house and found nothing.

It couldn't hurt to have another look.

9911 CONROY ROAD, 8:30 P.M.

Jess thanked Lori for the ride home. Dr. Martin Leeds, the Jefferson County coroner, would begin the autopsy on McPherson tomorrow. He couldn't guarantee he'd have a look tonight. Jess missed Sylvia. She hoped Nina would be found soon and safe.

The sound of yelping and thumping drew her weary attention to the stairs leading up to her apartment. The puppy half ran, half tumbled down the stairs. He didn't stop until he plowed into Jess.

"Hey, fella." What in the world was she going to do with this animal?

The BPD cruiser was parked in its usual spot. It was almost dark and Dan wasn't home yet. She'd spoken to him on the way home from Scottsboro. He was worried sick about Nina. Jess hadn't been able to reach Sylvia. She could imagine the Baron family was terrified.

"You look tired."

Jess whirled to face her landlord. "George." She summoned a smile. "I am. I really, really am."

"You've been working a lot of long hours." He pushed his glasses up the bridge of his nose.

"I have. We're on a big case." She imagined he'd seen the news.

"I didn't know you'd gotten a dog?"

Jess winced. "He's not mine. I don't know where he came from. He just showed up at my door last night."

"Would you like me to take care of it?" He shrugged. "Call Animal Control?"

"Oh no." Jess shook her head. "We're trying to find his owner." A frown furrowed its way across her brow. "Do you mind if he stays until we find his owner? I can pay a pet deposit if you'd prefer."

He waved off the idea. "I don't mind as long as he doesn't keep digging up my flowers."

Oh Lord. Jess hadn't thought of that. "He dug up some of your flowers? I'm so sorry. I'll reimburse you."

"No real harm done," George said. "That's what puppies do. They outgrow the urge eventually. No need for you to worry. You should rest. You work too hard, Jess."

"Thank you, George."

Jess couldn't wait to shed these clothes. As she unlocked her door, she glanced back down to the driveway. She hoped Dan would be home soon.

Inside, she let the puppy explore. She armed the security system then stripped off her clothes and headed for the shower. She needed to wash away the smell of death and the chill of uncertainty.

She piled her hair on top of her head with a clip. The feel of hot water sluicing over her body was almost enough to chase away the ghosts. Five or so minutes of pure pleasure under the water and she worked up the energy to wash her body. Fortunately, the morning sickness wasn't plaguing her now the way it had last week. She still suffered with a touch of the queasiness and the fatigue, both of which were normal, according to her doctor.

As she dried off, she refused to think about Amanda or her father or Maddie. She refused to let Spears invade the peace she so badly needed tonight. A little down time with Dan was exactly what they both needed. She peeked beyond the bathroom door. She wished he were home already.

After pulling on jeans and a tee, she wondered what to do about food. She wasn't really hungry though she knew she had to eat. It was too late for a real dinner. She wasn't in the mood for pizza or Chinese. She poked around in the kitchen. There was milk and eggs. A fresh loaf of bread waited on the counter. Somewhere in the cabinet next to the fridge there was cereal. She could have cereal and maybe Dan would like eggs and toast.

The puppy stared up at her, his head cocked in question.

"Hope you like Cheerios." She poured a pile on the floor for him. Since he gobbled them right up, he clearly didn't have a problem with boxed cereal.

No sooner than the milk hit the Cheerios in her bowl the chime sounded, warning she was about to have company. She checked the monitor. *Dan.*

Bowl in hand, she hurried to the door, sloshing milk as she went. The puppy followed, lapping up the spills. She disarmed the security system and released the locks.

The smile he gave her had her melting inside. "Man, it's good to be home."

Jess set her bowl on the coffee table and scrubbed her hands on her hips. "I've been worried about you."

Dan pulled her into his arms and since the puppy had stretched out on the sofa, he carried her to the bed. He settled there with her in his lap. "We're not going to talk about investigations. We're going to finish what we started last night."

The sound of stoneware crashing to the floor had them both scrambling off the bed. The puppy had knocked the bowl of Cheerios and milk off the coffee table.

"I guess we're still dog sitting?"

Jess winced. "Cook is trying to find the owner. No luck yet."

Dan sighed. "I should take a shower."

"Still no word on Nina?"

"There's been no ransom demand. Nothing."

Jess grabbed some paper towels. "It can't be Spears. Nina doesn't fit the profile." There were plenty of others who didn't but they were chosen for their connection to Jess. A connection didn't exist between Jess and Nina. She stopped, turned around. *Except Dan.* "Oh my God."

Dan looked pale. "You think it's him."

She nodded. The urge to cry came from somewhere deep inside her. "If there's no ransom demand, it has to be him."

Dan's arms were suddenly around her. "We will stop him."

She nodded. "We will."

He drew back, looked down at her belly, and then put his hand there. "No more talk about this tonight." He managed a weary smile. "This baby is counting on us to make the right decisions so I made a decision today." He dropped down on one knee, withdrew a black velvet box from his pocket, and opened it. "I don't want to waste any more time, Jess. Let's make this official. Will you marry me?"

Jess tossed the paper towels. Her hand went to her mouth. The ring was beautiful, far too extravagant, but absolutely beautiful. The tears were scalding her cheeks and she wasn't sure she could speak. Finally, she managed a nod. "Yes."

The puppy bounced over and sniffed the box as Dan removed the ring and slipped it on her finger. He stood, pulled her against him and kissed her so softly, so sweetly, she wanted to cry all over again.

When he came up for air, he murmured against her lips, "We could put the dog in the bathroom."

"Or we could go in the bathroom."

"Good idea."

With a bowl of water on the floor and the puppy busy having the Cheerios and milk he'd scattered over the floor, they slipped into the bathroom. They stripped off their clothes. He took the clip from her hair and let it fall around her shoulders. Her arms went around his neck, her legs around his waist, and she pressed her body down onto his. She cried out with the incredible sensation of being filled by him.

Dan carried her to the nearest wall and braced there. He kissed her face and throat, her shoulders. She touched his face, aching at the injury still healing on his forehead. She could have lost him. How did she make sure that didn't happen? Before the worry could take hold, he found her breast and closed his mouth over her tender nipple. Then he started to move. She came immediately.

He brought her to that incredible place again before he came, too. The next thing she knew they were in the shower. He washed her so gently. She did the same to him. By the time they dried each other off, they were both too weak to speak.

When they went in search of something to pull on, the puppy decided he wanted to join them. Jess laughed as she dragged on her favorite tee. She didn't miss the hint of a smile at one corner of Dan's mouth as the dog nipped at his heels.

Her cell clanged. Maybe Leeds had decided to have a look at McPherson's body after all. *Harper.* Jess frowned. "What's up, Sergeant?"

"Vernon called. The only things on Henshaw's iPad were countless searches on Spears and you. Nothing else."

Another dead end. "Anything else?"

"I also spoke with one of the evidence techs from the McPherson scene."

"And?" Jess's instincts went on point.

"His boots have that tread that picks up everything. The techs said the cracks were filled with dirt."

"Dirt?"

"Lots of dirt. They're checking on construction sites in the area. That's all I have for now, but I thought you'd want to know. I'm thinking maybe McPherson was doing some investigating of his own on the Brownfield farm."

"Could be. Thanks, Sergeant."

Jess mulled over the news as she picked up the bowl the puppy had licked clean. She fished the spoon from under the sofa and teased Dan as he mopped up a puppy piddle with paper towels. She made peanut butter sandwiches instead of eggs and toast, grabbed a couple of bottles of water, and they collapsed on the sofa.

"We used to eat these all the time in college." Dan licked peanut butter off his lip.

"And grilled cheese," she reminded him.

"Don't forget the Ramen Noodles."

She sighed. "Those were the days. The only worry we had was making the grade." The puppy tried again to jump up on the sofa with them. "No," she scolded.

"What's he been digging around in?" Dan grabbed his bottle of water and gestured to the pup's dirty paws.

"George's flowerbeds. It's a wonder he hasn't evicted me already."

"Puppies dig and chew. If you're thinking of keeping the dog—"

"Who said I was thinking of keeping him?"

"Just saying," Dan countered. "Puppies dig and chew."

Puppies dig. Jess frowned. "Why would an old dog be digging?"

Dan looked confused. "Why do you ask?"

"McPherson's dog had been shut out of the house when he was murdered. It's a German shepherd several years old. Lori thinks McPherson expected trouble and put the dog outside where he'd be away from the danger."

"What does that have to do with digging?" Dan stuffed another bite into his mouth.

"The dog kept running to the back door and then he'd go back to the middle of the yard and start digging. Whatever he was clawing at probably wasn't related to the killer." She scoffed. "There was no way anyone went into that backyard with that dog without shooting him first. But why was a dog that age digging?"

"Maybe he was trying to escape the fence," Dan offered.

"The spot he kept going back to was nowhere near the fence." She considered what she did know. "We searched the house even though Buddy had already searched the house and the building in the backyard and found nothing."

Dan held up a hand. "I'm going to pretend you didn't say that."

"He didn't find anything anyway and it's not like I asked him to do an illegal search."

"And if he had found something?"

"He didn't. Harper called and said the treads of McPherson's boots were packed with dirt," Jess went on. "Maybe McPherson buried something. Something important. That he didn't realize he needed to hide until recently. Like today just before he was murdered." She got to her feet as the idea formed more fully. "Maybe he knew he couldn't avoid what was coming and hid something. He put Roger out back to protect the dog as well as to protect what he'd buried. The killer wouldn't have any idea McPherson had buried something and, therefore, no reason to go into the backyard—dog or no dog."

"The dog may have been after a gopher or a ground squirrel."

"But," Jess narrowed her gaze, "what if there's something important to the case buried there?"

Dan sighed. "I take it we're going to Scottsboro."

"I have to go." Jess found her cell. "I'm calling Harper."

"Call Hayes, too." Dan stood. "And we'd better warn Foster so none of his deputies show up and shoot us."

TUPELO PIKE, SCOTTSBORO, FRIDAY, SEPTEMBER 10, 1:01 A.M.

While Lori made another pass through the house and Hayes inventoried the small building McPherson had used as an office, Harper and Dan did the digging. Jess held the flashlight.

"Whatever he buried," Harper said, "he did it recently. Dirt's soft. Not packed at all."

"That explains the dirt in the tread of his boots." Jess itched to get a shovel and help but Dan assigned her flashlight duty.

The hole was approximately three feet in diameter and every bit as deep so far. Old Roger had dug all around the perimeter but he'd been too distracted by all the activity at his master's house to stay on task.

"Wait." Dan tossed his shovel aside and got down on his knees in the dirt.

Jess tried to remember if she'd ever seen him in the dirt like this, T-shirt all sweaty, leather work gloves on his hands. Despite the circumstances, she smiled. Daniel Burnett was such a good man. Who else would come here in the middle of the night with her and then scratch around in the dirt because she had a hunch?

God, she loved this man.

Dan tugged a black garbage bag from the ground. Jess hoped it wasn't a dead animal. This whole exercise might be nothing more than a waste of time.

Both men removed their leather gloves and pulled on the latex ones Jess passed their way. Harper held the bag open while Dan removed the contents.

At the first glimpse of brown file folders, Jess's pulse kicked into high gear. She went down on her knees and opened the first of four thick folders.

"It's his Brownfield case files." Anticipation had her heart thumping.

"Let me hold that for you." Dan took the light from her.

"What's this?" Harper pointed to the corner of something white sticking from one of the folders.

Jess tugged free a white business size envelope with her name scrawled across the front. Inside the envelope was a handwritten note.

Deputy Chief Harris,

I followed the Brownfield family for most of my career. I was considered a close friend by Amanda's grandfather. I had all the evidence I needed to take down a multi-generational family of murderers—the first I'd ever encountered. Then I made the same mistake your father did. I got involved with the daughter of one of the most evil monsters on the planet. Even after the monster was dead, there was Amanda. She loved killing just like he had and Margaret loved her daughter too much to give up on her. I tried to make her see but I couldn't. In the end it was that love for her daughter that killed her. The last part of goodness in me died with Margaret.

You asked me for the truth and I wasn't willing to give it to you. I can't answer any questions about your father. Margaret refused to speak of him except to say the truth was locked away and the key was lost. If I'm already dead when you find this then I was right about the dark-haired man in the black Infiniti who's been tailing me. Watch out for him.

Mac

Jess reread the note. Maybe the last part of goodness in McPherson hadn't died. She passed the note to Dan. "I knew he was back."

"Who?"

"The dark-haired man. I think I saw him outside the Redmont Hotel." So he was the one doing Spears bidding the past couple of weeks, including taking Amanda to him. He was probably the bastard who had put her in that river. Jess hoped she would have the opportunity to take him down.

With Harper's help, Jess skimmed through the reports and photos in the folders. It took some time, but she couldn't stop. Reading over her shoulder, Dan held the light.

"McPherson was keeping an unofficial file of what these people were doing," Harper noted.

"Jesus Christ." Jess reached his final conclusions. "Old man Brownfield and this Mooney character killed people for sport." She turned to Dan. "Not for marketable goods or food. For the pure pleasure of hunting them down like animals." Jess shuddered. "McPherson believed Margaret was a victim."

"He was in love with her," Dan countered. "Maybe he didn't want to see who she really was. She may have been the one who kept the cops off her family."

"The distraction," Harper suggested.

"She made it hard to see the truth." Jess agreed. Every good hunter had a decoy. Dan passed the note back to her. She read it again. "Margaret said the key was lost. Do you think she could've been talking about the key found with the reverend?"

"Sergeant," Dan said to Harper, "let the others know we're closing this down and going home. Ask Foster to get someone over here to secure the scene. This evidence can be logged in later this morning."

"Yes, sir."

Dan took the note from Jess and placed it with the files. Then he closed his hands around hers. "Are you sure this battle is worth the price?"

Jess felt that old familiar elephant settle on her chest. "No." She shook her head. "It's not worth the price. Not at all."

"Then I say we go. Disappear for a while and let Gant and his people do this."

Jess wished it were that simple. "There's no way to escape him, Dan. You know that. He'll find us wherever we go. We have to finish this."

Dan nodded. "You're right. We don't have a choice. What we need is to get lucky."

"I'll try to make that happen," she promised.

She'd been lucky a few times in her life. When she met Dan...acceptance into the Bureau. Finding Dan again.

This time she wasn't waiting for luck to make up its mind whether to shine on her or not. Jess intended to make her own luck.

CHAPTER TWENTY-ONE

"I decided to postpone the surgery."

Lori stirred in the seat next to Chet. "Sorry. I dozed off. What did you say?"

"I think I should postpone the surgery until this is over." Spears was way out of control. No way was Chet going to be out of commission when Lori and the chief needed him most.

"Where are we?" Lori stared out the car window.

"About forty-five minutes from home."

She relaxed back into her seat, but she was staring at him. He could feel her eyes on him. "Is postponing the surgery what you want to do or what you think you should do?"

He laughed. The woman knew him too well. "I can't say that I want to postpone, but I think it would be best considering the way this Spears situation is going."

"You have a point. It might be a bad time for the team. We can't always put work first, Chet."

He glanced at her. Wished he could see her face better. Had she really just said that? "Can you repeat that for me? I think maybe I heard wrong."

She laughed. "I'm trying to think like a person rather than a cop. Jess and Burnett have put work first their entire careers. Look how long it took them to piece a personal life back together and now everything's going to hell. I don't want to waste all that time."

"Hey, did you see that rock she was wearing?"

"I did. I wanted to ask her about it but there wasn't time. He must have done the official proposal last night."

"I guess he wanted something to celebrate after being forced into administrative leave. Talk about a crappy day."

"Hayes said Nina Baron went missing. You think that has anything to do with Spears?"

Hearing her say Hayes' name tightened Chet's jaw. He'd warned the guy he better watch his step. "I haven't heard any of the details."

"According to Hayes she disappeared from the top private facility in the southeast. The senator is pulling out all the stops to find her and to get to the bottom of how this happened."

"Looks like Chief Black inherited some major headaches."

"I have no sympathy." Lori stretched. "I guess I'll be clearing the Brownfield murders off the case board today."

"Yeah. The feds will probably oversee the ongoing removal and identification of the remains. It's one-hundred percent their mess now."

"We know Henshaw, Mooney, and his girlfriend were murdered by Spears's follower, but there are still pieces that don't fit."

"Who knows how many followers we're dealing with here. There could be dozens working under our radar." That was the part that worried Chet the most. The enemy could be any sick bastard who'd gotten an invitation to the game from the Player.

"It's hard to fathom how far Spears was willing to go in this crazy quest to dig up all he could from Jess's past. Some parts were news even to her." Lori shivered.

"When you have those kinds of resources you can make things happen." Chet wanted Spears dead. He wanted his son back and Lori safe.

She was watching him again. "So you've made up your mind about the surgery?"

"It's the right thing to do. We need to be focused on staying safe right now and stopping this piece of crap."

"Okay. As soon as we can breathe again, let's get back on the surgeon's schedule. I don't want to risk our future children."

He pulled her close and kissed her forehead. "You got it."

She leaned on the console, resting her head on his shoulder. "We're going to have to talk to Jess about Hayes."

"Either that or I'm going to end up kicking the guy's ass."

"I don't understand why he's turned into such an arrogant ass. He actually told me that Jess wanted me in Scottsboro the other morning. He told her I wanted to go because there was something I wanted to check out."

"Did you ask him about it?"

"Yeah. He said there was a miscommunication. No big deal."

Chet shook his head. "I can't figure out why he thinks he needs to stick so close to the chief. She's already made it clear that we're a team."

"Who knows? If he doesn't realize by now he can't move ahead with her that way, he's an idiot."

"You know, I saw him come out of Burnett's office the other day. Do you think it's possible that Hayes is working for Burnett? You know, keeping an eye on the chief for him?"

Lori didn't answer for a bit. Thinking it over probably. The idea could be a stupid one.

"I think you're onto something. Burnett pushed his transfer paperwork through." She shook her head. "Son of a bitch. That's why he feels comfortable being so cocky even with Jess. He knows Burnett has his back."

"If the chief finds out, Hayes will be out."

Lori hummed a worried sound. "That could cause some major tension between her and Burnett. They don't need that right now."

"So we keep this to ourselves?"

"For now. We're basically theorizing anyway."

"You're right. The chief has a lot on her plate right now. She and her sister were pretty torn up about the DNA news. They're both worried about that little girl."

"Poor kid. She's got a bumpy road ahead of her."

"Yeah." Chet hoped his son would grow up recognizing and appreciating how lucky he was to have parents who loved him more than life.

"You know what I find totally bizarre about the Brownfield case?"

Chet laughed. "You mean besides all those dead people being buried in the yard?"

"Besides that," Lori acquiesced.

"Tell me."

"Margaret, Amanda's mother, had an affair for years with Jess's father who was married. Then later, she has a long-term affair with McPherson, also a married man—at least in the beginning. What did these two men have in common besides wives?"

"Her affair with McPherson was about protection. She didn't want her father to go to jail at his advanced age. Later, it was about keeping Amanda out of jail. Having her own personal ABI agent to keep her family's extracurricular activities covered was a major coup."

"What about Jess's father? The woman never married. It was as if her purpose in life was to serve as a conduit for drawing protection to the family."

"But the chief's father wasn't in law enforcement. He was some sort of salesman."

"Was he?"

Chet braked at an intersection and met Lori's gaze beneath the glow of streetlamps. "You might be on to something."

"We should dig around. See what we can find before we approach Jess."

"Where do you suggest we start?"

"Buddy Corlew."

Chet harrumphed. "Good luck finding him. Corlew seems to be missing, too."

CHAPTER
TWENTY-TWO

Jess hated to leave Dan at home. It felt wrong. She'd barely slept after they'd gotten home. Once she'd started going through those files she couldn't stop. Her father's name hadn't come up in any of McPherson's reports. He'd documented murders going all the way back to Amanda's great-grandfather. According to his calculations, Amanda was the first female killer of the family.

"Lieutenant Hayes is here." Dan looked from the window to Jess. "You hardly slept at all. You could wait and go in after lunch."

She grabbed her bag and managed a smile. "I'm fine. I should turn these files over to Agent Manning and see where this leaves our investigation. We'll be focusing on my mother's journal and Henshaw's ramblings today. I'm hoping his notes will lead us somewhere besides a dead end." A frown tugged at

261

her brow. "What about you? I hate leaving you here like this."

"I have a lot to do. I'm having lunch with Dad. Looking at more houses. Maybe I'll drag him along."

Jess hugged her arms around his waist. "That's a very good idea. What about Katherine? Won't she want to come along?"

"Mom and some of her friends are helping Mrs. Baron today." Worry slipped back into his eyes. "I feel like there's something I should be doing, too."

Jess hugged him tighter. "The senator will have the best out there looking for his daughter, but if you feel you need to help, then you should. House hunting can wait. You and your dad go help out where you're needed most."

Dan nodded. "I'll check in. See what I can do. Nothing official, of course."

"That won't matter." Jess smiled up at him. "Being there will."

"I love you, Jess." He looked deeply into her eyes. "Please be safe out there."

"Promise." She tiptoed and kissed him. "Love you, too."

Dan walked her down the stairs to meet Hayes. Leaving Dan standing there watching her go made her chest hurt.

"Nice ring," Hayes commented as he guided his car onto the street.

"Thanks." Jess admired the engagement ring Dan had given her. It was gorgeous.

"We headed to the office?"

She thought about that for a moment. "Before we go to the office, I'd like to drive by the Irondale house. Have another look around."

"Headed that way."

She searched for her cell. If Sylvia needed anything, Jess wanted to do what she could. She made the call, but it went to voicemail. Jess urged her friend to call if there was any way she could help. There was probably something more she should say, but Jess had never been very good at that sort of thing.

If Spears was involved with Nina's disappearance, what in the world could he have planned?

This game he was playing had taken several startling twists and turns from his usual MO. His obsession with Jess had become his singular goal. Rather than abduct and murder her as he did his other victims, he had set her up as an equal challenger in his game. Of course, he fully expected to win—he was a sociopath—but he couldn't resist upping the stakes against himself.

If Jess had her way, his obsession with her would be a fatal error.

BIRMINGHAM POLICE DEPARTMENT,
9:05 A.M.

The call ended and Lori turned to Chet. "That was Jess. She and Hayes are headed to the Irondale house."

Chet looked up from his laptop. "I guess we stay on the Henshaw investigation."

Lori nodded, frustrated. "Where's Cook?" He hadn't come to the office and hadn't answered when she called him in the middle of the night about going to Scottsboro.

"Maybe he's helping Dr. Baron."

"I should try to call him again."

"Maybe he was out partying last night." Chet shrugged. "Too early for him to know anything on the exam to celebrate."

Before Lori could put through the call her cell vibrated. *Corlew.* Surprised, she hit accept. "Hey, Corlew, what's up? Where have you been? The chief has been trying to reach you."

"Listen up, Lori, I got a situation. I need back up fast but I don't want Jess involved in this."

Lori tapped speaker. "I'm here with Chet Harper. Chief Harris is in Irondale. What's your situation?"

"I don't have time to explain how this came about so you're going to have to trust me on this, okay?"

"Let's hear it," Chet said, his skepticism showing.

"I'm sitting across the street from a house on Argyle Drive in a Red Mountain neighborhood. I'm texting you the exact address right now. I've been staked out here for forty-eight hours and I now have visual confirmation that Spears is in the house."

"What did you say?" Lori needed to confirm what she thought she'd heard.

"I repeat, I have visual confirmation that Spears is inside the house."

Chet reached for his phone. "SWAT can scramble in—"

"Don't call anyone," Corlew cut him off, "except Burnett. If Spears has a source inside the BPD we don't want him getting a heads up. I need Burnett and you two. No one else. You keep Jess out of this. It's too risky."

"She's not going to like it," Lori warned.

"Just get here," Corlew urged.

"Calling Burnett now," Chet assured him.

"Okay. We'll do this your way," Lori relented. "Just don't do anything reckless, Corlew."

"Can't make any promises, sweetheart."

The call ended. Lori tried to calm her racing heart, wasn't happening. "I don't care what Corlew wants, I should call Jess."

"Let's see what Burnett says. We can make a call to the chief en route."

It would take them at least twenty minutes to reach Corlew's location.

If he had Spears cornered…this nightmare could be over soon.

TWENTIETH STREET SOUTH, IRONDALE, 10:00 A.M.

Jess wandered through the house that had been her childhood home. No matter that it was falling down in disrepair now, she could still see each room as it had once been. The living room with its comfortable furnishings, and the kitchen with its delicious smells and her mother all smiles fussing over her latest baking creation. Down the hall were the two bedrooms, the first being the one she and Lil had shared. The walls were no longer pink and the cute rug that once graced the floor was long gone. The sounds of laughter and her mother's voice whispered through her.

Funny, she didn't hear her father's voice. Was it because he was gone all the time with his job?

Fury swept through Jess. Or had he been visiting his other family—the one that somehow got him and their mother killed.

She tried hard to reserve judgment until she knew the truth, but part of her hated him already. The pain she and Lil had suffered when their parents died, the myriad of foster homes—all of it was his fault.

Jess gathered her composure. "Let's go, Lieutenant."

She had seen enough.

"Excuse me a moment, Chief." Hayes stepped to the other side of the room to take a call.

As the lieutenant's hushed tones echoed in the room, her attention settled on the message Spears had left here for her two weeks ago.

Welcome home, Jess!

He thought he had her right where he wanted—confused and off balance. He was wrong. Yes, she wanted to learn the truth about her parents' death, and yes she wanted to know why her father did the things he did. She would look for the answers, but if she couldn't find the truth she could live with it.

Her life now, with Dan and the baby, was what mattered. Today and tomorrow and every day after that. This rotting house and the past she had no power to change were no longer important.

Spears could take his game and go to hell.

"We need to go, Chief."

The urgency in Hayes's voice jolted Jess from her unsettling thoughts. "What's going on, Lieutenant?"

"That was Chief Burnett. He's with Wells and Harper. They're providing backup to Corlew."

Dread welled in her chest. "What kind of backup?"

"Corlew has Spears cornered. They're going in."

How was that possible? Worry and confusion joined the dread. She would know if Spears had been found, wouldn't she? "We need to get there, Lieutenant. What's the location?"

He shook his head. "I don't know."

"What do you mean, you don't know?"

"Burnett wouldn't say. They're doing this off the grid to ensure there's no leak. No one else knows about the op. No one."

Emotions whirling like a hurricane inside her, Jess grappled to put what Hayes was saying into prospective. Was it possible this nightmare was about to be over?

It could be just another distraction Spears had set in motion…or a trap.

DEPRAVED is coming November 22! Order your copy now exclusively at Amazon! Then, it's down to the wire for Jess and her team in the shocking two-part finale coming December 26!

Don't miss any of the Faces of Evil books already available! Look for OBSESSION, IMPULSE, POWER, RAGE, REVENGE, RUTHLESS, VICIOUS, AND VILE!

CPSIA information can be obtained at www.ICGtesting.com
Printed in the USA
LVOW11s2254190115

423534LV00001B/11/P